MY ALIEN WARRIOR

Rotha mates of Xavia | Book Four

REVERIE HARWOOD

MY ALIEN WARRIOR

Rotha mates of Xavia | Book Four

REVERIE HARWOOD

Cover design by Mayhem Cover Creations

For those ready for a different world

Chapter One
Love Line

Layla

Welcome to Xavia, ladies.

Captain Smith's slick voice slipped into my dreams before my eyes could watch the video on loop. In my stasis pod, I woke feeling heavier than rocks.

You've been chosen to save this planet in a genetic exchange. We will be back in one year.

I was dumber than rocks, too. No one was coming to disconnect me and hand me a margarita. This wasn't the long, exotic vacation I won in a social media contest. It was trafficking. My cousins warned me, but it was sponsored by our government. I didn't think they had the balls.

I yanked on lines and limbs until I untangled and exited the fancy coffin for my tiny private room on the spaceship. In the wall, the helpful welcome video repeated. In the mirror, I was me, but different. My skin looked great. The bags under my tired brown eyes disappeared. Six months of sleep and hydration did wonders. My curly brown hair was both greasy and frazzled. Nail clippers and scissors sat at the sink. I cut my nails, which had grown too long for a Midwestern working woman like me. I tossed the tools into my personal bag. Who knew if I might need them.

I shouldered the bag before stepping from one of many rooms like mine. We'd been part of a large spaceship, but now the hallway opened cleanly with a ramp into the vibrant purples and pinks of an alien jungle. Xavia.

The women gathered as a crowd. A brunette told a trio of Xavians of the contest and the video. Their muted yellow skin showed they were female. Their eyes widened, their pupils swirled. The emotive remained the same—shock.

"You are not volunteer colonists?" They asked in English before rushing outside to confer with her group.

Outside, the males of their species gathered. The government hadn't lied about them. They were green, horned, handsome, and hopefully helpful.

"Do we have any food?" I asked. I had packed sunscreen and bikinis, not ready-to-eat meals.

All the women shook their heads. They'd packed similar things. We got a count of heads; twenty-nine of us.

The Xavian women rushed in. They towered over us. "We have to go now. An Orkain is coming."

"A what?"

"They didn't tell you about the Orkain? They've driven us to near extinction."

Without food, we didn't have much of a choice. We followed her.

Nope, the government hadn't mentioned giant flying feathered demons. I'd have remembered that bullet point.

A Xavian with bright eyes guided me to tree cover.

"Stay with me," I pleaded. Did I smell cinnamon?

"I can't. I must fight." He rushed against the flow of people.

The pod teetered with the Orkain's weight as it ripped through the interior. A scream from inside rattled my bones.

Number thirty. Fuck.

The giant beast dragged a limp, bloody woman from the depths of the ship. Someone pulled on my arm.

"Come with me. I'll take you to safety," he said.

I followed the stranger into the jungle. They had learned our language. Did they have a place they intended us to stay?

"I'm Layla."

"I am Moto."

SIX MONTHS LATER

"Layla's Love Line," I joked, answering Moto's video communication device. There wasn't much demand for accountants here, but I'd become an adviser for our group of refugees.

Human Sara laughed from the settit screen. Behind her, Xavian Vance looked confused. This power couple with matching hair-dos didn't need my help. Sara was living proof that humans could experience rotha—a fated, physiological forever-love relationship—with Xavians. Faint swirls marked their arms. I'd seen them in person and still marveled that this existed in our genetic code.

The Xavians didn't pressure us, but they gave us opportunities. Handsome, polite, eligible bachelors hosted us separately. Some women showed signs of rotha. For others, Sara created Switching Day. Sadly, her sister was determined to switch.

"I can't get her to change her mind," Sara complained.

Katy and Drex might have problems, but they also had chemistry. They flirted tons during the broadcast of Sara's and Vance's kumirata/wedding. Even if Sara couldn't convince Katy to stay, she determined where she went. Sisters were sneaky. I wish I had one.

"Who will be her host?"

She smiled. "Chelk. They will not get along. Drex will need a temporary guest too."

Sara needed a safe placeholder while Katy came to her senses.

"Why are you messing with this? Does she have rotha marks?"

"Not yet but it's rotha. They just don't know it yet."

"Rotha marks usually form later. Sara and I were the exception. Before then, it's more internal. You can sense your rotha mate's presence and find them in the jungle. You yearn for them, and they for you." Vance said, squeezing his Sara.

Yeah, that was something that Moto and I didn't share. I'd gotten lost so many times Moto had to establish rules. Moto had done so much for me. We were polite friends with no chemistry. We weren't rotha mates.

Hosting a human had been a serious proposition for him. He had learned English. He wanted a partner and a family. And yet, he had forced none of that onto me. Instead, he taught me about Xavia and kept me safe. Like Sara and Katy, he deserved to find his rotha mate. I'd sacrifice more than a few nights to give him a chance at rotha too. I'd move in with Chelk.

"I'll do it if someone comes to stay with Moto."

Sara broke into a grin. "I've got just the one. Her name is Dani."

She had already thought this through, huh? She was a sneaky cupid.

"Might work for you, too," she encouraged.

"What does Chelk do?"

"He's a warrior, a soldier in the Xavian Guard."

"Oh, you don't say?" A handsome soldier, huh? I'd made that mistake before…I looked forward to meeting him.

Chapter Two
Human Women

Chelk

Human women were the worst.

Stella hated my home, trapped with my screaming baby. She'd prefer to fight the Orkain herself, and she did. Over the last moons, she found her place and moved in with Vjann, leader of the Xavian Guard.

Switching Day brought Katy, and Katy brought tears. Had she cried for six months, or was this a new condition? If the prince didn't please Katy, I had no chance. We were supposed to get to know each other, and didn't yet know about Rixo. She'd sob more then.

Drex mentioned she ate morning meals, so I prepared one and left it in the hallway with a brief announcement. Unwatched, she might emerge as a timid creature. I waited all day. She made no noise. *Did she even use the bathing room?*

I cooked the most extravagant dinner. Before the Orkain's arrival, I was a chef in the public house with my mate, Kaytor.

Now I set the tiniest public house table and stared into the dark hallway. Stronger than I'd ever been, a shut door gave me pause. At her door, her morning meal swam in spilled drink.

I knocked. "Are you going to eat dinner with me?" Anger punctuated each word. She wasted food? Ungrateful...

Silence. I expected my toddler to act this way, not an adult.

"You're being rude, you know?"

She said nothing.

My hands cut through the air in my aggravation, landing on nothing. A silent shout wretched from my body. No wonder the prince had shrugged her off onto me. I'd had more positive interactions with Orkain. There was nothing to work with here. I made a mistake holding any optimism for Switching Day. Disappointment hit hard. I should have refused a guest.

How were we going to build any trust if Katy hid, leeching from me? Her people were traffickers. Could I trust her with Rixo? I rested my head against the door. She at least needed to eat.

I replaced the food. I didn't want her to hunger or fear hunger. She didn't have to eat with me. I packed food for Gulshan and Rixo. Maybe I could see Rixo before he fell asleep.

* * *

The warm and humid air kept me well hidden from the Orkain's heat vision. I ran too fast, slipping and using foliage to keep me upright. I arrived at Gulshan's with a sweat, a rapid heartbeat, and ready to see my son. He fought to open the door as wide as his smile.

"Hah-zah!"

The sweet boy hadn't forgotten me yet. I scooped him up, kicking the door closed.

"Wet!" he squealed, swinging past my attempts to clean the crusted remnants of food not sourced by me. He swiped crumbs into his long bangs. Should I cut it or tie it? Kaylor would know. They had the same wispy hair. He didn't have horns yet, just little nubs underneath. Otherwise, he was a miniature me—handsome and stubborn.

"Home?" he asked. No, but I'd be here until he fell asleep. Gulshan disappeared as I took over bathing duties. It took many to care for a child. I couldn't do it alone. Gulshan was a seamster. Everyone's clothes and armor suffered when he chased around Rixo.

Wrangling my son and putting him to bed, singing him a song in my raspy voice as he fell asleep felt *right* even if it wasn't in our home. I shouldn't have stayed so long, but my mind felt in a better place. Gulshan gave encouraging parting words.

"You're trying to do the right thing."

During the run home, I wondered which *part* was the right thing. I'd tell Katy more about me and Rixo through the door if needed.

Inside my quiet house, the food remained untouched. I knocked on the door, receiving no answer. Not even shuffling.

"Please let me know you are safe. I am worried about you."

Nothing.

"I'm coming in if you don't say something. Hello!?"

I opened the door. My caution turned to panic. No one was inside the nest of blankets on the bed. How long had it been empty?

Fryyre.

The bathing room? No, not there. I rampaged through the house, searching the interior and the exterior. She was gone. Dumb. Dumb. Dumb. And embarrassing—What should I do? I had to call someone. I rationalized Vance organized the switches and should know this one had gone awry.

Vance answered the settit after delay and with displeasure.

"What is it?" He panted and wiped his forehead.

Prince Drex arrived soon after, marching through my house and into my face. His eyes spun fast and intensely.

"What happened? What did you do to her?"

"Me?! What did *you* do to her? She's been hiding since you left her. You care? You didn't even say bye to her."

"When do you think she left? When did you last hear her?"

I shrugged my shoulders. I didn't appreciate being stuck in the prince's complicated love life.

He cared—he got here damn fast. He rampaged through my house. At least Rixo wasn't home.

"She's run away. She's done it before," he said, satisfied she was gone. He ran off without further instructions.

I wasn't the first Xavian to lose this woman. I wouldn't lose my life for it either. They could be idiots, but I had a son. Humans were too much trouble.

I ended up outside like an idiot anyway.

Drex found Katy and killed an Orkain. Vance needed help to retrieve the corpse. We couldn't chance waiting until dawn. If the Orkain recovered it, we'd lose our chance to study it.

"There's no way he killed it." I stopped.

Our lanterns cast dark shadows against feathers as long as my arm. Hocked legs crumpled underneath the bulky, lifeless terror. Its horns, torso, and arms were like mine, but the feathers not. I kneeled with a crunch upon one of its wings and traced my hand along the wound between the wing joints. He'd stabbed it from above—how do you get above a winged giant?

Two idiot lovers ran out into the jungle, and instead of recovering their bodies, I was viewing a massive victory. Our first single battle was won. Drex had killed an Orkain that threatened his rotha mate.

This was rotha love.

Vance and Sara might have rotha marks, but the Orkain murder convinced me. Rotha between humans and Xavians existed. Both those idiots were dead without it. That's why Kaytor was dead…

I twisted its horn to see its contorted, wicked face. Orkain had killed my mate, hurt my child, and decimated my village. I wanted to pluck, gut, and butcher this corpse. Destroy it like they had destroyed us.

"Come on, let's do this," said Vance, more subdued than usual. Did he have the same idea, or did he just want back home to his rotha mate? No matter.

We dragged it, its carapace making a nice sleigh against the moss and mushrooms on the jungle floor. Vance dislocated its arm pulling. I still had a grip on its horn. Its neck at a satisfactory odd angle. Knowledge of how to kill these creatures changed our tactics.

"Would you accept Layla as your guest?" Vance posed a different tactic.

Another human? Did my home not have enough chaos? Something about dragging a corpse through the muck and darkness loosened my tongue.

"Why? Because I've done such a great job with the first two, or because it'll free up space in Drex's home to make and keep a baby?"

Vance chuckled. "I guess the second."

The number of English-speaking eligible bachelors must be short. Would Layla bother to talk to me? Whatever. We'd survive the next six months, and I'd have an excuse to stop trying.

Layla it was.

Chapter Three
Hi Rixo

Layla

A wave of giddiness hit me. Anticipation was always the best part…far better than reality. There were so many possibilities, and they all unfolded to this moment—meeting Chelk. *Deep breaths. In and out.*

Katy called me into the living room where my packed bags sat. Time to meet my Prince Charming. Well, not *Prince*.

I smelled fah and something like hazelnut. Hopefully, Katy hadn't prepared drinks. I wanted to unpack in my new home and get to know my new…

Fuck, he was handsome. Gorgeous. Katy stifled a giggle. Did I gasp? I hoped I didn't gasp.

His jet-black horns curved with the golden ratio touted by dry scientists and classically trained artists. Who cared about ratios when thick dark hair tousled them? The occasional wrinkle around galaxy eyes betrayed an age that his otherwise puppy face screamed.

Tall as the prince, he gave an awkward bow or curtsy. Katy's smile bubbled to the surface again.

"Haellea," I said, releasing him from his cracking knees.

He returned to full height, towering over me. His size was intimidating.

"Are you going to run away too?"

Point-blank. "I hope I have no need. My name is Layla. I'm looking forward to getting to know you."

"I know." To what extent he knew, I wasn't sure. Katy had been quick to say he was handsome and nothing else. What did she not tell me?

So much for polite introductions. I wanted to rub my hands on his ridiculous pectoral muscles, which wasn't a polite introduction either. His tight-fitting shirt revealed bulging muscles across his broad shoulders. He didn't skip leg day either. Big monster thighs. Despite his evident strength, I carried no fear. Domestic violence was another unknown atrocity on Xavia…only demons in the sky.

I dismissed guilt for my attraction. My government had chosen good qualities in me to victimize. I reminded Katy as much. Still, half of my goodbyes were raised eyebrows of *He is so hot!*

Then, I followed Chelk out the door to our new future. He didn't let me carry a single thing, which became necessary. Our path was hardly a path. I needed both of my hands to fight the jungle. He stayed close so his bulk and my luggage could keep the brambles off me. He showed me each foot and hand placement. So much for carrying on a conversation. This was a hike! What Chelk thought of me, I couldn't read at all. He was quiet. Stoic. I'd crack him once we were safe inside.

I tired before we reached a door tucked into a knoll. No wonder Katy had gotten lost.

"I will need you to knock on the door…and perhaps carry the child," he said, taking the moment to shift my luggage in his arms.

Why did I need to knock—wait, what?

"We're picking up Rixo." He kicked at the bottom of the door, trying to knock—the first thing I'd been asked me to do. I knocked. The second—?

A squeal came from inside and stomping. Little fists banged on the door from the other side—somewhere between the height of Chelk's kicks and my knock. Chelk's child.

Behind the long legs of a remarkably old Xavian darted a tiny, remarkably young Xavian. He fought past me and my luggage to reach Chelk, his dad, who crouched to his level. He hugged his dad's face before turning around to eye me, head to toe. I smiled. He didn't. I was a stranger. An alien.

"Haellea. What's your name?"

Chelk translated my question. The little one boldly stepped out from between his dad's legs to answer.

"Rixo!" he shouted with an infectious giggle.

"Haellea Rixo." I patted my chest. "Layla."

"Lala."

Damn. Lala? How cute was that? Hella cute. So was the kid. Chelk's features softened in Rixo. He had huge starry eyes and little horn nubs sticking from his dark, messy hair. I hadn't seen a smile light up Chelk's entire face.

If Chelk smiled like that, I wanted to see it.

Chapter Four
No Time

Chelk

Layla kneeled to Rixo's level. He wasted no time in diving his tiny fingers into the spirals of her hair. His fingers tangled, and he pulled.

She didn't panic. Her eyes remained deep and still. She untangled him with a smile. I regretted asking if she was going to run away. She wasn't dumb like Katy. Stella held Rixo only when necessary. I expected more of the same, not this stunning, gentle woman connecting with my son. Relief turned to grief. I missed her.

"Kay-tee?" Gulshan asked.

"No, not Katy. This is Layla." I said, embarrassed. *Had the foyer always been this small?*

"And Rixo is yours? And who is this?" Layla asked.

Questions fired from both directions in different languages.

"Gulshan is the village seamster. He helps me with Rixo, but Katy used up your time." Neither Gulshan nor Rixo knew much English. Only I experienced the full awkwardness of everyone learning of each other's existence.

"Ooh! A seamster? Did he make Sara's kumirata dress? I wanted to know…" Layla started.

Gulshan perked at the word, *kumirata.* He chattered atop her. I didn't catch it.

"Kaytee," shouted Rixo as he circled the newest human. Hopefully that was less rude in her culture.

"Time to go. Thank you." I said to everyone and no one in particular.

I leaned to my right, lowering my body for Rixo. He climbed onto my shoulders using Layla's luggage as footholds.

Everyone said haellea. With a quick check of the skies, loaded with luggage and a toddler, I led us home.

"I can carry him," Layla offered behind me.

I didn't have to translate for Rixo. He launched into Layla's arms. I didn't have time to argue. The sun would set soon.

"So, they didn't tell me you had a kid," Layla shared, her hands full.

My laughter bit into the air. Of course they hadn't. They didn't tell me I was going to host three different victimized humans either. "That's Vance for you. I don't think he planned this far ahead. You can stay with us for as long as you desire, but yeah, I have a kid."

"Does he need someone to take care of him?" she asked.

"Always. They need constant supervision at this age. Oh, but you're asking about yourself? Yeah, I figured you might help."

She wasn't with the prince anymore. She was with a lowly warrior and a single dad. I was sorry I couldn't devote myself to her. Hadn't she done labor with Moto? At least childcare was inside and less dangerous…probably.

"Oh," was all she managed. Rixo patted her cheek.

"We can work somewhere else for you to stay more to your desires. Vance should have communicated who you'd be living with—Rixo and me."

She thought for a moment. "No. Thank you for hosting me."

I refrained from asking if she was going to run away now. I'd sleep against the exterior door if needed.

"It's just Rixo and you? What happened to his…your…?"

"Kaytor died by Orkain many moons ago." Kaytor was more than Rixo's mom or my mate. She was life, abundant.

"I'm sorry," she said. Her eyes lingered on the scar on Rixo's forehead.

Surviving on Xavia had been difficult. Jealousy, grief…maybe something new…wrestled inside me. I shook the thoughts from my head and brought my attention back to protecting these two.

Behind me, Rixo loved his new friend and babbled, telling her his life story and the life stories of his favorite toys. Neither of them spoke much Xavian, but they shared an enjoyable conversation. I translated for them occasionally, relishing the simple vocabulary. I refrained when Rixo announced he'd soiled his diaper. She'd figured it out. Her tiny nose scrunched and her voice pitched higher when she caught the scent, but she didn't complain.

Besides the full diaper, I dropped her bag in the mud trying to help her. I promised to clean it after changing Rixo.

When we arrived, I dumped her things into her room and pried Rixo off her. There was no point in giving a tour. The homes were all the same. She'd probably pout in her room like Stella and Katy did. I apologized for messing up her bag.

Whatever Gulshan had fed Rixo, he'd turned into a brown horror. I kept a hand on him at all times to keep him from running into Layla's room half-naked and half-clean. He kept darting his eyes to the door. Despite his short memory, he remembered her. He liked the new person in the house.

I didn't blame him. I distracted with silly faces, nonsensical noises, and bribes, but could barely secure the diaper before he slipped from my hands.

"Rixo, leave her alone," I called out before giving chase.

Too late.

He swung open the door. Layla was bent over. Her big, round, pale ass was bare for me and Rixo to see.

Layla screamed. I apologized, although whether I remembered to say it in English, I wasn't sure. Rixo shrieked in happiness before realizing there was drama afoot and began sobbing. I was in shock myself. Why was she naked? My heart pounded. I tried not to think about planting my face in her big, gorgeous ass or what colors it turned when slapped.

Shaking my head did nothing to clear my thoughts. I shouted another apology for Rixo and me over my shoulder.

Fryyre, I messed up. Saw her undressed…she was never coming out of that room.

Chapter Five
Embarrassed

Layla

Rixo's laughter echoed down the hall. Thankfully, his father's laugh didn't join. How embarrassing. I was sticky and sweaty from the hike. I wanted to change. Oh my God, that was neither proper nor cute.

I finished dressing with my foot against the bottom of the door and listened for tiny impending stomps. I knew toddlers. He'd be racing to repeat the ruckus, excited by the attention he'd received. I needed a lock.

"Lala!" Rixo shouted when I reappeared in the living room.

He ran over and hugged my leg as if they were best friends and had been apart for a long time. As opposed to having just met and it being bare a few minutes ago. Rixo hugged me with unexpected warmth. Laughter bubbled from me. My government must have found the perfect mark. I had no prospects on Earth, so toss me, love-starved, into a broken home.

My face felt warm for multiple reasons when I saw Chelk, arms crossed, watching his kid and me interact. His musk was spicy and warm. *Did I smell okay?*

He apologized again.

"There's no lock on the door."

"I'll replace it tonight. I removed the locks as soon as Rixo could reach them." Chelk said something to Rixo, then translated. "He's going to show you his toys while I cook dinner."

Chelk disappeared into the kitchen. I sat on the floor as Rixo brought me toys one-by-one—wooden blocks, soft stuffed toys, and lots of shiny stones. He ordered his toys by a metric unknown to me before kicking them down the hallway. I lined up softer toys for him to toss.

Chelk's home had a familiar layout, but with more toys, smaller clothing, and toddler-height marks on otherwise bare walls. There were no photographs of Kaytor or infant Rixo. Had they lived here together?

Was Chelk an eligible bachelor? He'd had a mate and lost her. Rotha was for life. Moto's parents died within days of each other. Chelk and his mate were young, though. If he survived for Rixo, I understood. Rixo had my heart, too.

"Let's throw these instead of rocks." I offered him a stuffed toy which looked vaguely like a cat. He accepted the toy and threw it before picking up more rocks.

I pointed to different colors and named them in English. He told me them in Xavian, but I wasn't sure how much I should rely on a toddler for my language skills. I should learn. Chelk could teach us.

Delicious smells drifted from the kitchen—nothing I'd experienced from Moto's kitchen. He steamed the vegetables he grew. Once a week we'd trade for meat, and he boiled it. This—*this*—was more like cooking! Spices and oils. Like home.

"Let's go see what your daddy is doing." I offered Rixo my hand, unable to stay away.

In the kitchen, the stove and oven blared heat. Three dishes competed for space on the stove and dominance in the air.

"It smells fantastic!"

"Fantastic is good?" His devious smile revealed that he knew the answer.

He minced onions, sweeping them into one pot, before shaking another pan of vegetables with skill and sizzle I'd seen on television. Where else did he have skills?

He routed the pan of hot rolls from the oven underneath my nose and high over Rixo's greedy fingers. They were finished with silky caramelized onions. From the large, heavy pot, he dished meat and vegetable stew into shallow bowls. Perhaps he only cooked to soften the food for Rixo, but I delighted in the unexpected meal. What else did this husky, handsome warrior hide?

"The last pot has sweetened apples for dessert."

Mm, dessert?

Chapter Six
Fantastic

Chelk

I didn't know the word *fantastic*, but hearing it from Layla's lips elated me. I hoped to impress her, starting with a home full of delicious smells. Fantastic smells, apparently. Maybe dragging the stove from Frustnerdd public house hadn't been a mistake, even if it was too large.

I scooped Rixo up and placed him in his highchair and pulled out the farther chair for Layla. Rixo's face scrunched up with the seating arrangement. He wanted to sit next to his new friend. I gave him a roll to pummel while his stew cooled.

Layla pushed her curls behind her ears and blew on a spoonful before tasting.

"Oh my, this is delicious. Very good."

"I used to run the public house in Frustnerrd."

"Is that like a restaurant?" she asked.

She described people at many small tables, ordering from a large menu. At the public house, I cooked one enormous meal each night and served it until it was gone. People sat together even if they didn't arrive together. And while I had a handful of regulars, no one requested an individual meal.

"The invasion shut the public house down, and I got recruited to the Xavian Guard."

"When did you have Rixo?"

The comforting aromas faded with my appetite. "After the invasion but before we evacuated Frustnerrd."

We hadn't meant to bring a child into the world as it was changing. It had changed so much. Rixo wouldn't remember his mom, but he wouldn't remember her death or his scar's origin either.

"Well, the food is delicious. And is this a mushroom? Moto doesn't grow these."

"They grow wild," I prided myself in collecting food while out. I didn't have time for many heshiev plots.

"I think I've painted them."

"Painted?"

She scurried to her bedroom and returned with a sheet of thick paper like I'd never seen. On it there were blobs of color which bled into the others.

"The paint was wet. I brushed it on and when it dries, it looks like this."

"This was your job on Earth?" If I squinted my eyes, I saw a Xavian abode—likely Moto's—and the surrounding creep of the jungle. I recognized the brown blobs as the 'mushrooms' in question, but wasn't a photograph easier?

"No, I was an accountant. I worked with numbers."

She snatched it away. She didn't want Rixo to touch it with his stew-fingers.

"What do you mean worked with numbers?"

"Well, numbers representing people's and company's money. I helped them keep track of their money."

Oh, currency. We used little currency even before our population loss. We mostly traded in goods and services.

"So, you lost your job too?" We had that in common.

"Oh yeah, I guess you could say that…"

I wanted to ask what she meant, but I felt childish questioning everything. Then she giggled at my actual child.

Rixo squished the vegetable fibers with his tiny fingers before smearing it on his shirt. I sighed. He couldn't play outside much and there weren't other children his age. I'd allow him to play with his food.

Xavia, as I explored carefree, town to jungle to waters, was no more. I hated Rixo didn't have that. Despite that, dinner went well. Rixo enjoyed his captive audience, laughing and performing.

After-dinner was back to chaos. First, he vomited—on Layla. Sickness only increased his energy levels. He ran around, making it difficult to clean…anything. I'd had him for a few hours and he didn't even keep down the food I'd given him. My appreciation for Gulshan dissipated as I realized Rixo must have slept all day. He was a whirlwind of energy.

"Woo!" he shouted.

Woo, indeed. It was easy to remove Rixo's clothing. Hold the garment, not the child. Getting clothes back on him was harder. I stripped along with him and got in the shower with him. I got plenty wet anyway if I didn't.

"Lala," he gurgled as I washed his chin.

"Yeah, you like Lala, you like every Lala," I said. His world was a revolving series of caretakers.

I popped a bubble to his great delight, and I saw Kaytor. Even though Rixo looked a lot like me, I saw her in Rixo's saddest and happiest expressions, adding grief to every intense emotion.

I turned off the water and turned on Rixo's favorite part. He delighted in the warm air that dried us. His hair had gotten longer and moved in the wind. I separated his body from mine so that we'd dry entirely.

When the dryer ended, he whined to get down. He wanted to play and delay bedtime. He was also naked. Nope, nope. We weren't about to run naked into Layla's room. Playtime became fight time as I got a diaper and shirt on him, and pants on myself. I carried him to our room we'd share for the next six months.

Reunited with toys he hadn't seen in many days, Rixo forgot his rush to leave. I followed his commands, holding things he gave me and surrendering them upon command. After he pulled every single toy from the chest, he sat inside and declared he was hungry. I bet he was; he couldn't have gotten much from dinner's temporary stay. I pushed him into the living room in his makeshift cart. There, he found another level of energy, running around and otherwise ignoring the food I gave him. It had been a setup. My son threw toys and destroyed any semblance of tidiness I attempted for my guests.

Layla entered with smiles and energy for Rixo. They ran around the house together, more easily than my bulky frame managed. When bedtime came, so did the tears. When I picked him up, he'd settle. Back into the crib, he'd cry.

Hours later, he slept in my bed. I cautiously slipped out to find Layla had retired to her room. I tried to dismiss my disappointment.

Oh, the lock. I'd do that tomorrow.

Chapter Seven
New Morning

Layla

In the morning's quiet, I unpacked my art to decorate my new room. Disney princesses burst into song and threw open dusty curtains. I had windowless, bare gray walls and hosts I didn't want to wake. I hummed instead. *Would Chelk mind me painting a window on the wall?* My paintings hadn't impressed him. Not surprising. I wasn't Rembrandt.

Ready for my morning beverage, I ventured from my bedroom. In the living room, Chelk sprawled on the urish, asleep. He looked as uncomfortable as you could be while remaining asleep. One of his legs hung over the side.

I kept watch over him as I crossed through to the kitchen, not wanting to disturb him. I located the matches on the wall and lit the oven and kettle burner. His kitchen was better organized than Moto's. I measured fah from a dusty can in the cabinet into a mug and put it into the oven to warm.

Waiting for the water to boil, I checked on Chelk to make sure he was still sleeping…and shirtless. His hard pecs rose and fell with his breath—okay, with his snores. Even his snores were manly and fitting, calming and safe. His pants were loose, but with one leg off the couch, the fabric tightened over his large and intimidating package. *Of course it's big, he's big. Get over it.* Still, the thought of them springing out of his sweatpants interested me and scared the crap out of me. I'd never seen one, much less—maybe the girls were lying to me—three.

The sound of the water boiling behind me brought me back to reality. I pulled the mug out of the oven and poured the water, watching the petals' final bloom, swirling deep purples and ambers. With my nightgown as oven mitts, I carried the steeped goodness back to my room. At Moto's, I would have sat on the lanai, but I didn't want to panic the tired dad. His question rang in my ears—are you going to run away too? I sat on the wooden chair by the matching desk and got lost in the petals' dance awhile. It always brought a smile to my face.

I set up my dwindling paints. If I wanted more, I'd need to make them. I'd made natural watercolors before, but I didn't recall the exact recipe nor was I on the same planet as the sourced ingredients. The medium was a ratio of gum arabic powder, honey, and hot water. I purchased gum arabic powder from an art supply store, but it originated from the gum of a tree. Did Xavians have honey? The new art excited me.

I was here to try new things, right?

Chelk was new. Something inside me bubbled and burst into a smile. A warmth settled below my navel. A small child wailed. I changed quickly, not wanting to repeat yesterday's show, and stepped out.

The living room was empty and the bedroom door was shut. I prepared a mug of fah for Chelk. He might need it after his night on the couch. Did he sleep there every night?

The bedroom door opened with a bang. Chelk's disagreeable noises confirmed a jailbreak.

"La-la-la-la!" Rixo cheered as he padded through the kitchen with his three tiny weens out.

Aw, he remembered my name.

"Good morning, Rixo." I called as his tiny butt disappeared past the counter.

Chelk sauntered into the kitchen with a diaper and pants draped over his shoulder. I smiled stupidly at his sweatpants.

"Is this not appropriate?" he asked, gesturing at his bare chest. "I'm not wearing shoes, either."

"Oh, no, it's fine. You're just…it's fine," I stumbled through the words.

"Have you seen a small person come through here?" He asked, leaning on the doorframe.

Goosebumps sprang across my chest. Rixo waved frantically. Straight-faced, I stalled.

"Oh, uh, describe him for me."

I pulled the mug out of the oven and poured steaming water into it.

"He's *this* tall, fast. Green butt."

I laughed. "Why do you know the word *butt?*"

"Oh, I had to—the explanation is lengthy and inappropriate."

"It's a long story," I supplied.

"What is?"

"No, it's a saying on Earth. 'It's a long story.'"

"You'll have to tell me."

The way his eyes spun made me wonder if he was messing with me. I offered him the cup.

He frowned and made no move to take it.

"It's fah. It's the one thing I know how to make," I said.

"I hate fah."

"Sorry." I said, sad our cheerful banter had slowed.

Why have something you hate?

Oh crap. It belonged to Kaytor.

"I'm sorry," I said again.

"Haellea!" shouted Rixo, his little head bouncing into view from the counter, desperate for the attention to return to him. I was thankful for the distraction.

"No, I've just got to dress this little one!" he shouted as he picked up the half-naked boy and raised him high in the air before tossing him onto his shoulder.

My smile lingered with Rixo's distant shrieks and giggles. What to do so much fah? I didn't want to waste it. Both fully clothed, Chelk returned in leather-like chaps and a grim look. Something was up.

"Can I prepare something for you or Rixo?" I asked.

"No, but Rixo will be hungry later. I've been called into work."

My eyebrows and panic levels rose. "You can't leave him here with me. I don't know how to take care of an alien child."

He arched an eyebrow. "No? You've been doing a fine job."

"No, I'm not comfortable with that just yet." Fear twisted inside of me.

He thought for a moment. "I can take him to Gulshan's today. You will go too."

He shouldn't order me around. "What did Stella do when she lived with you?"

"Stella usually trained with us." He chuckled. "But Rixo was younger, slept more. Gulshan needs more time for his work."

"Does Gulshan dye his own fabric?" Rixo's bright purple shirt was the same shade as Sara's kumirata dress.

"He does. You could ask him about it."

"Okay. I'll go."

I tucked samples of my paints to show Gulshan. They sat thick in my pocket, and Rixo wanted to take them out. I offered the game of putting *more* things into my pockets. Rixo enjoyed the game and brought me many things, one at a time—keeping my little secrets safe.

Chapter Eight
New Training

Chelk

Decaying Orkain waited for no one. I'd already seen it, carried it, dragged it, but if Prince Drex said Come, then we must. He was big-headed, and he was our prince. If the prince said Train, then train we would. I hoped his confidence would not lead to deadly mistakes.

Rixo didn't want to leave home and cried explosively. He struggled in my arms, eager to be in Layla's arms or maybe to run home. I didn't give him the chance. No way was I chasing him through the jungle this morning. The walk to Gulshan's was slow with Layla in tow.

Gulshan waved us in with raised eyebrows, his sewing project in one hand. He still wore his muumuu.

"I didn't expect you back so soon," Gulshan said in Xavian.

Rixo led Layla around the living room for a tour. This was his second home.

"Neither did I, but Drex called us back. Too quick," I stressed. "You can scope her out. Make sure she's good with Rixo."

Hosting Layla gave us a minuscule chance of a more stable home with two parental figures, but I couldn't force childcare on my guest Day One. She had a point about her and Rixo being difference species. I felt I was running in circles and getting nowhere fast—and I was late.

I shouted goodbye to Rixo. He'd gotten a good night's sleep and hopped around. He'd already forgotten about me.

"I'm sorry. Thank you," I said to a grumpy Gulshan. Hopefully, he'd gotten some good sleep as well. "Tell Layla I said haellea."

Gulshan grumbled and his muumuu swished as he closed the door. I wasted no time, taking off toward the meeting, but it didn't matter. I was already late. When would I get it together? So much was demanded of me. I used to control my life, spending the day cooking and choosing ingredients and ratios. The public house didn't have a set schedule. I cooked when and what I found fit. As a soldier, I had no choices. They modeled the military after our primary school days, as if we could go back. Except now they trained us to fight.

I caught whiffs of acrid sweetness, but the stench was undeniable at the meeting spot. It was risky to bring the corpse here. Maybe the other Orkain could find it. Our meeting place was secret, deep in a jungle canopy but with an area large enough for the remaining Xavian Guard to fit.

The Xavian Guard circled with Prince Drex and the dead Orkain in the center. I sidled beside Kane in the last row, tilting a horn to him in haellea.

"Late," he informed me.

Yeah, no shit.

His glossy black plaited hair reminded me I hadn't brushed mine. I ran a hand through it, catching on knots. Despite our similar heights, Kane looked down from his bulbous, crooked nose, broken in many battles.

I hadn't missed much. I carried that awful corpse before it cooled. I had intimate knowledge of its rough feathers, massive clawed feet, and horns. With a booming voice and puffed chest, Drex explained how he had defeated the Orkain.

Its abdominal plates were thick like a carapace. No wonder our arrows glanced off from below. It weighed even more than it looked. How it stayed in the air, I didn't understand. However, the other side of their body held weaknesses—feathered wings and joints in its spine. Blood pooled where Drex had dug in knees and heels into the beast—determined and intense to hang on. Here, blades could penetrate and devastate. Blood hardened in the back of the neck, above the wing joint. I recalled its blood cooling in my hand. It tightened into a fist.

"With this new knowledge, Vjann is developing new training which you will start today."

Something was different about him. He had a new, quiet confidence from heroic violence and rotha. Did he think we could win this war? At least we would train rather than charge in. Around me, the same confidence was growing—an excitement. Drex had opened the door by killing an Orkain, and everyone was ready to step through it. I remained cautious.

Stella was absent. Perhaps training had been an excuse to see Vjann. He wasn't one for speeches, and he barked his commands.

"We are forming into teams of three, each member with a different role—leader, base, or flier."

He shouted our assignments from a list and our roles. Kane's eyes churned when he heard my name. He'd be my leader.

"Oh great, these assholes," said Lian as he sidled up to us.

I chuckled. If he could fly like words flew out of his mouth, he'd be fine. He was young and hadn't filled out yet. Looked even younger with his pale hair and skin. I had more desire to protect him than to throw him onto an Orkain.

As a big guy, I was a base. I'd carry a big shield to launch a flier into the air and onto the Orkain. Leaders maneuvered the Orkain into position and were a mishmash of personalities. In size, Kane burgeoned between leader and base. However, his agility won out. Kane could roll on the ground and jump, like he had been launched. I hoped he'd take more of a "bait" rather than "lead" approach, but fryyre, I'd throw him up onto Orkain if need be.

Lian took to the air like a bird, one of our highest fliers. He was young, and I wasn't sure how he'd handle actually landing on his enemy and driving a blade into it. I'd have no trouble. I was old enough and wise enough, had seen everything taken away from me. However, I was too big to be a flier. No one could lift my ass.

Lian and I quickly preferred the smaller shield board. He had to aim his foot at a smaller target but it gave me more control of his launch. Also, less surface translated to a faster launch. The fliers shoulder-rolled out of it, or my favorite—landed on leaders. Fliers needed to practice their grabs and stay on long enough to deal the fatal blow. Kane thought little of either of us. He eyed other teams he considered more competent or talented. He'd rather be part of an elite team than help me and Lian.

Launching our youngest and smallest wasn't a great strategy, but I didn't have better one. Would we survive long enough to get over ourselves and become a helpful team?

I wasn't training to have doubts.

Chapter Nine
Agi, Agi

Layla

Gulshan's home was a large barrack for many of the bachelor Xavian Guard. Rixo raced through the long hallway dotted with private rooms as if it were his own home. Gulshan was the oldest Xavian I'd met with bushy eyebrows, wrinkles, and sharp eyes. He murmured his surprise in Xavian under his furrowed brow.

Gulshan had taken over most of the living space with piles of fabric scraps and clothes to be repaired. Of two styles of clothing, heavier, plainer fabrics required by soldiers pushed aside softer, more colorful fabrics. Gulshan scolded any efforts I made to tidy. Apparently, he had a system to his madness. While I didn't approve of the messiness, I enjoyed seeing things being created, made, repaired.

The vibrant purple fabric from Sara's dress was a recent project and stood out among the others, though. I pointed to it.

"Did you dye this fabric?"

"Kumirata?" He snatched the fabric and pressed it into my hands. His eyebrows rose and disappeared underneath his dark horns.

The ceremony to commemorate rotha? As if.

"No kumirata for me, no," I replied. "I want that color for my paint."

I offered my small painting. Gulshan gushed, admiring the paper, the paint, and the art.

"Cuhlure is dansk." He rushed to the settit and opened images I recognized as Katy's photography.

I almost hugged him. This was perfect. Katy had documented the entire dyeing process, from picking berries which Gulshan called Dansk to mixing them in a bowl with hot water and dipping the fabric. This was perfect. I'd have to remember to send a message to Katy thanking her if this worked.

"Where can I get Dansk?" I asked. Moto hadn't taught me that plant.

Gulshan picked up his sewing again. "Dansk during the wet season."

"Oh." I deflated. That made sense. Sara's kumirata was months ago. I considered the plants in season. Could I extract the pigment from the very plants I wanted to paint?

Rixo wailed as he stomped in, holding his finger. Gulshan put down his sewing to tend to him, but Rixo presented the offending injury to me. I examined the finger and found nothing. Still, I made reassuring cooing noises and rubbed his back until either the pain subsided or he got bored. He stopped crying, took me by the hand, and began pulling me to the other room.

Gulshan had a satisfied as he picked up his sewing. At least I had passed the babysitter test. Gulshan accepted me. I didn't know where I stood with Chelk yet. An uneasiness filled my stomach. I distracted myself by playing with Rixo and keeping him out of Gulshan's hair. I could at least do that.

Rixo paraded a couple of blocks in front of me. He could have been explaining Xavian Shakespeare to me, but I had no reference point. I offered to stack them by stacking them. He knocked them over and became utterly delighted by the result.

"Agi Agi," he said, which was a command to repeat whatever had just occurred. Toddlers were universal in their love of repetition.

I stacked one block on top of the other and reached for a third before he knocked it over. He stamped his feet and clapped his hands with joy. Just wait till he saw three blocks. I adored him.

Gulshan ate simple raw foods like Moto. Rixo slobbered on a softened root vegetable while playing with the rest, much like his blocks.

"Agi agi urish" Rixo yelled to be thrown on the urish. He ran. I threw. He ran back. I didn't know where the giggles ended for one round and started for the next. He seemed heavier despite not eating anything. My complaining only added "Hevee" to become "Agi agi urish Hevee" as the changed command.

He bubbled. I kept at it. I'd been alone on Earth. Here there were even fewer people. But Rixo—this little dude loved me very much.

My cheeks hurt from laughing so much by the time Chelk arrived to take us home. Eight soldiers returned with him, and the loud house got much louder. Everyone returned, thankfully. It must have been a training drill.

Rixo was excited to see everyone, and it was tough getting him to go home. Then he complained about being separated from me on the walk home. It was nice to be wanted, but his father struggled with him. In just a few minutes, Rixo was falling asleep in his father's arms. Chelk jostled him, but it was no use. He'd been rocketing around Gulshan's all day. If Xavian toddlers were like human toddlers, this nap would power him through the rest of the night.

Chelk took long strides, unencumbered by his sleeping child.

The path wasn't straightforward and required small climbs and descents, but I gained familiarity—more than with Chelk. While it was hard to hike and talk, I tried my best. He confirmed Dansk berries had fallen, but he showed me the tall bushes. I told him about apple picking with my cousins in the fall.

"Did you have any siblings growing up?" His childhood might be a safe topic.

"I had two younger sisters. They're both gone."

"I'm so sorry."

There wasn't much joy in his history. I understood

"I was what they call a rainbow baby. The baby before me didn't survive, and I wasn't supposed to either. I had health problems. I didn't have any siblings, but I had a lot of cousins. We spent summers on my grandparents' farm, running around barefoot."

"Children ran a lot here too—*until.*"

"What was that like?" I struggled to picture it.

"What does it matter?" Chelk spit.

I swallowed, hesitating. "It'll never be the same, but what if the Orkain leave or you defeat them?"

"We'd move back into the towns. I'd work as a chef."

"That would be wonderful."

Chelk only coughed in response. Was I too optimistic? Wasn't that the point of the Xavian Guard?

"Even if you don't get rid of the Orkain, there are still lives worth living."

Rixo ran around in circles inside, but it wasn't the same as experiencing terrain and sunshine and streams. Maybe he could run around on Earth. Could they come back with me? "Would you ever take Rixo to Earth?"

His movements became stiff as he thought. "No. I can recognize the predators here. On Earth, they walk among you as humans. If your government treats you poorly, how much worse will they treat us?"

He had a point. We hadn't made the best impression by trafficking our own to this planet. The Orkain were a straightforward enemy. Humans, very much not.

I admired Chelk and his efforts to help his people and his son, even if he didn't have high hopes for their future. I felt safe with Chelk. Was there a way I could show my appreciation?

Chapter Ten
Experimentation

Chelk

Rixo's slumbering body weighed heavy in my arms. Life here might be difficult, but I would not take him to Earth. I didn't trust her people.

He slept through the hike. Even when I put him in his crib, he didn't wake. My arm's extensions released a soldier's stench. I'd been traipsing through the jungle, launching Xavians into the air, handling decaying Orkain today, and it showed. Maybe Rixo had been knocked out by it.

Layla was waiting for me in the living room. Great. And there wasn't a cute kid to distract from my poor hygiene.

"I'm going to wash," I told her before heading to the bathing room. Had I felt this awkward with Stella? No.

Once in the bathing room, I peeled off my leather chaps and tossed them aside. I turned the water temperature up high, much higher than when I showered with Rixo. The hot water relaxed my tired, tense muscles. The long day of training and of being someone's ramp took its toll. I scrubbed fast to get back to my guest in a more pleasurable condition.

With regret, I turned off the water, ran the dryer, combed my hair, and put on a pair of linen pants. I needed to get to know Layla. Gulshan said I needed to stop bringing over Layla and Rixo. My commanding officer reprimanded my tardiness. Everyone pushed their ideas onto me. None of my decisions seemed my own. Poor Layla didn't deserve that. Neither did Rixo, though he was too young to understand.

To her credit, Layla wasn't hiding in her room like Stella or Katy. Instead, she'd spread out a bunch of her papers and paints on the low table by the urish. She bent over them happily. She had bowls of water and food that she'd smeared onto paper. It looked like an activity Rixo would enjoy.

"What are you doing?" I asked. I sat close as I dared.

She pulled a curl back behind her ear. "I'm experimenting. Trying to create watercolor paints."

I examined one chunky smear. She wasn't painting with food, was she?

"That's going to rot" and attract bugs.

"I don't want to make art from food, just extract the color. I agree though—not the beans." She scrunched her tiny nose even tinier. "Do you have honey on Xavia?"

"What's honey?"

That launched into a huge discussion about bugs on her planet that spit a sticky, sweet substance that humans eat. They were like cows she milked, but tiny. What would be similar on Xavia? I didn't understand why she didn't use Xavian art supplies. Didn't she want to stay here?

When Layla angled the paper she worked on, another caught my eye.

"What is that?" I asked, moving to pick up the painting.

Layla's tiny elbow came up to block me, but I dragged it with a finger. The mild, watery green face didn't look like Rixo. It was an imaginary child, a blend of our two species.

"Nothing," she said, her voice high-pitched. She neatened the papers back into a stack. "I was just playing around."

She picked up her water cup to put away.

"What is it a picture of?" I pressed, moving to pull it out again. Why wouldn't she show me?

"No!" she swung around and into my knee.

With her hands full of jars, she dumped water onto the urish on either side of me as she fell onto me.

Even as I attempted to right her, I appreciated the way her ass looked divine over my knee. The thought of slapping those round cheeks pink and red hardened my cocks. I picked her off my lap and onto her feet. She now held empty jars. Water seeped through my pant legs and I jumped up myself.

Layla's eyes widened at the watery mess. She looked ready to burst, her cheeks reddening. I didn't want her to wake Rixo. That'd be worse than a wet urish. I put a finger to her lips. Static electricity zapped between us.

Her eyes lit up. She mouthed she was sorry. I enjoyed watching her lips, but I tore away from them to go get a rag, or three. We blotted water from the cushion. Layla kept apologizing, but it wasn't her fault. I pushed too far. The urish would dry. I had a toddler and was used to messes.

I didn't dare step into the room with Rixo sleeping in it. He'd just wake up and neither of us would sleep. I'd sleep on the floor next to the urish before I ruined the opportunity.

Layla figured as much when she offered.

"Well, I guess you'll have to sleep with me," she said.

My cocks shifted in my pants disrespectfully. Fryyre.

Chapter Eleven
One Bed

Layla

"Well, I guess you'll have to sleep with me," I said.

The offer tumbled out of my mouth before I could think it through. I had spilled so much water on the couch where he slept. I'd do the same for any of my friends on Earth. And this wasn't even my bed. He had given it to me, and I could share it. Except I'd never shared a bed with anyone.

Chelk tilted his head to the side. His eyebrows rose at the suggestion.

"I mean, if you promise not to touch me."

"I cannot promise that," he replied. "What if I roll in my sleep?"

I laughed. "Incidental touching is okay. I just mean this isn't an invitation to mess around."

"Mess around?"

Ugh, the language barrier was real. "Like, no sex."

"Right, a place to sleep." He ended with a yawn.

We finished cleaning up, silent with the impending one-bed encounter. He was stoic and hard to read. He didn't try to look at my paintings again. Maybe I overreacted, but I didn't want him to see *that one*. I'd just been messing around with my green paints. A pale green inspired me to blend human and Xavian facial traits. Rixo held him. It was a whim, but it was embarrassing to be found out—like, I was writing his name repeatedly in my notebook. For the record, I didn't have a notebook.

I'd ruined our evening. We were both dead on our feet and there was nowhere to sit not covered in kid-stuff or my watery mess. He should sleep. I worried about him using weapons or sparring, or whatever he did in training. It was a dangerous job.

My heart pounded in my eardrums as we went to bed. I slipped underneath the blanket farthest from the door, hinting he was only welcome so far.

The paintings on the wall were my favorite ones. He didn't seem to notice them. Instead, he stood looming, unzipping and pulling his pants off his hips. I shivered under the blanket.

"Oh no, no…" I hissed.

"What? They're wet." He asked, eyes swirling.

Oh, right. "Well, keep your underpants on."

"As you wish," he said, amused.

I averted my eyes and soon he was sliding underneath the blanket with me. The bed was over-sized for me but not for its builder. Suddenly, it seemed much smaller. Even though we didn't touch, I was acutely aware of his presence, his weight on the bed. I fought to stay on my side, his side creating a gravity well. He would be delightful to cuddle, though now he pitched a massive tent.

I coughed. They were massive and pulling in my direction.

"You have my word. I'll stay on this side."

Just because he stayed on that side didn't mean his dicks would. His bulky shoulders and the thickness of his legs were mountains to be scaled. He was the epitome of sex, super masculine. My heart pattered with nervousness. I was the timid virgin, worried about his size.

His steady snores soon filled the room. I wasn't years-deep into childcare, and could not fall asleep so quickly. I watched his handsome shapes rise and fall. Would they fit?

Chapter Twelve
His Lockdown

Chelk

So much for getting to know Layla last night. All I'd done was get an embarrassing erection and pass out. Next to her, all my tension dissipated (or, more likely, moved to my dicks) and my body—given a moment's rest—took it. The sleep was divine. And the waking was just as strange. As my eyes adjusted, I took her in.

I was unaccustomed to having someone adult-size, much less an alien, next to me when I woke. Everything about her was different and provocative. Her soft, sandy-colored skin was smooth. Her face had no nubs or ridges besides her nose, mouth, and small eyes. Even when her eyes were open, they were so still—no spirals of light—just a black circle that got smaller or larger to adjust to light and the surrounding color of brown before white. Simple, pristine, and pretty sure always judging me.

Even the thought of her passing judgment didn't bother my cocks. They had no respect, half-erect, aware of how close we were to her. I was thankful to sleep in the bed. Stella had never offered, so I would not mess this up. If I were going to undress her with my mind, I wouldn't do it in bed with her.

So I got up.

Okay, it wasn't the most respectful thing to do. Even covered in blankets, her figure mesmerized me. Her soft shoulder and arm disappeared from sight. The curve of her hip, butt, and legs melted down into small calves and feet.

No matter how small or damp the urish was, I would not sleep next to Layla again tonight. She took a toll on my body. I was like a precocious teen. I stumbled for lack of blood flow. Annoyed and embarrassed, I left the room and encountered more annoyances.

Visible from the living room, the red glow of the settit signaled my least favorite lockdown—the one that included the Xavian Guard. Heat in my chest expanded through my aching, stiff body. Though it meant I had time with Layla and Rixo, lockdowns grated my nerves. I didn't like being told what to do.

The Guard must have spotted an Orkain. With our training so fresh, it was unlikely we'd be called in to use it just yet. Thus, the lockdown. Before I could get a handle on myself, Layla bounced into the room—from curly locks to toe.

"We're under lockdown," I complained.

"Oh, we can spend some time together! I'll make some fah. Are you sure you don't want some?"

"No." Her enthusiasm surprised me. Somehow enemies flying overhead did not dampen her disposition.

Layla prepared two mugs of fah. Had I answered wrong? I had gotten into the habit of drinking fah with Kaytor, but I stopped. I contented myself with being grumpy. Layla was excited and bubbled from the start. Unbothered being stuck inside, she hummed. She didn't need the extra energy, especially if she was going to run circles in my tiny place like a child. Buzzing around, she disappeared and returned with small utensils and paper. She sipped from one mug of fah and dipped a brush in the other. Placing the brush to the paper, she created brown streaks.

This again—*painting*. I gave her plenty of clearance, not wanting it on the urish.

"I'd love to get some other colors," she said as she layered color over what were maybe leaves.

Her leaves looked dead.

"When you go back to Earth, you'll be able to paint again."

"Sure, if I go back, but I want to paint now. I'm in such a beautiful place and I'd love to use that in my creative pursuits."

If she goes back? I noticed she hadn't brought last night's painting out.

"Katy does photography. She can take a picture for you."

"It's not the same. I don't know how to explain it. It's like a sense of ownership. I enjoy creating things. Don't you when you cook?"

Most of our food didn't need to be cooked, but I enjoyed creating new tastes. She dipped her brush in water and made lighter shades of the tannish fah. Would she dip her brush into lunch or dinner tonight?

Rustling preceded wails, and everything became about Rixo. He cried while I changed him and while I attempted to feed him. Every game devolved into throwing things and crying. Even Layla couldn't cheer him up. Layla took Rixo's tantrums in stride with absolute, endless patience, and it sort of pissed me off. In comparison, everything I did seemed like an overreaction, and I hated myself for each one. Maybe this was why my baby was the way he was. I needed to get my temper in check.

I was stuck in the house with this overactive, overtired toddler—anxious and unable to do anything about it. The Orkain were out there and I wanted to kill them, to rid the world of them, so that Layla and Rixo could go outside and play. With energy to burn, I got on the floor to do exercises. I had to maintain my physique while trapped in my small home, which only felt smaller when Rixo climbed on top of me. I supported my straight back with straight arms, while he crawled and hung from me. Layla watched from the urish, nearing fits of laughter. She didn't hide in her room. She was out here, watching us, engaging with us. I used Rixo as extra weight as I squatted and jumped. Unfortunately, nothing to full extension—the house was too small. I struggled to not hit my head. I hated lockdowns.

For lunch, I sauced some vegetables to pour over bread. Grinding the vegetables until they disappeared into sauce was the only way my child consumed vegetables, as far as I knew. Unfortunately, he spent most of the meal rolling the bread into hard balls.

"It's not *eating*, but at least he's spending time with his food," Layla offered with a sweet giggle that cut through me.

Unfortunately, I was a firm believer that food had to go into their mouths and spend some amount of time in their stomachs to count. And that was a win I felt like I didn't get often. Usually, Rixo ran around in circles until it would all come up, then would run in circles in the opposite direction.

Layla nibbled on the fresh vegetables I gave her. "Ooh, this one's sour! What do you think, Rixo?"

Rixo wanted to give his opinion, so he accepted the bite of food.

"Sour!" he shouted around it in his mouth.

But he didn't spit it out. I held my breath as he chewed and swallowed, still playing with the bread on the table.

Layla gave a sheepish smile, maybe also surprised it worked. Fryyre, she was a trickster…and better with my kid than with me. My heart buzzed inside me. Then it overwhelmed me.

I got up without finishing my food. I wasn't hungry.

This was too much…just too much like *before*. Those few precious months before it was all taken away from me.

I got up and cleaned the kitchen, leaving Layla to care for my child. Their combined giggling behind me cut through me, opening me and spilling my guts into the sink. It could be Kaytor and Rixo behind me. Losing her was the absolute worst thing that ever happened to me. I pushed down the panic to rush out the door and run.

If it hadn't been for Rixo, I would have wandered in the jungle until exposure or Orkain took me. I had to take care of Rixo…Kaytor's baby. If I couldn't save her, I could at least make sure the part of her that existed in Rixo survived.

I scrubbed at a dish that didn't need to be scrubbed, mostly to keep from snapping it in two. I would deal with this, just like daily life. Rixo needed me. Rixo needed others. That's why Layla was here. It didn't have to be any more than that. I was providing her with food, an entire bedroom, and for any need that might arise that she would discuss it with me. Layla was beautiful, but I wasn't obligated to engage with her in any romantic way. And that was the easiest way—the only way—to make this work. I had to tolerate people because Rixo needed others in his life. They'd already begun a relationship, falling into sync. I was becoming the odd one out, not sure how I fit in.

She liked Rixo, but I didn't know of anything that Layla *didn't* like. On lockdown? The woman was making art with her morning drink. She always had a smile, always had a reason to smile. She liked the food I made, and she laughed when Rixo made messes or asked for kisses. I was thankful that she got along with Rixo, but it would just make it that much harder when she left. At least he and Stella hadn't really bonded.

Was Layla going to stay on Xavia? She was from a different planet. This wasn't her life. In a few months she'd be back home and I'd be here with a screaming Rixo and another lockdown.

After lunch, Rixo began crying again. He would break her yet. I waited for cracks to show through her smile. He was an epic force, and going with the waves meant sometimes drowning. He was tired and needed a nap, and he wasn't about to fall asleep. The walls pressed in when I wasn't watching; the house getting smaller with each pass of my eyes and wail of Rixo. Rixo only had meltdown after meltdown all day. Why wouldn't he stop crying? Was he sick?

"His routine is off," she offered an excuse for him.

Routine. The routine where I wasn't here. If I thought Rixo needed more time with me, I was wrong. I was doing wrong no matter where I was. Maybe he'd go to bed earlier if he didn't nap now. There was at least that hope. He began screaming. Great.

This was miserable.

He swung a pull-toy around his head. In a moment it snapped, and he was in tears again. He threw the toy on the ground. With bulky fingers, I tried to retrieve the string from the toy. It did not go well. A piece that was not supposed to snap, snapped, and I took my turn to slam the stupid toy to the ground. I bit down on my tongues to prevent teaching Rixo a new curse word. He cried. I was losing my sanity.

"Let me try to fix it," Layla said, retrieving the heap from underneath me.

Without the toy to distract me, I was back to Rixo. I took a deep breath, picked up another toy, and offered it as a replacement. He took it from my hand only to throw it against the wall.

"That's why your toys are broken." I rubbed my eyes with big paws.

I should have gotten him some new toys before we got stuck here. Lockdowns were inevitable, but I never seemed ready for them. Half the time I didn't need to be; Rixo would be with Gulshan and I'd be doing something worthwhile, protecting my people. Instead, I was failing at being a good dad in my home.

I hated lockdowns.

Chapter Thirteen
Her Lockdown

Layla

I rescued the heap from the two guys and fished the string from the toy's interior reel. Rixo tossed the substitute and held his hands up toward my repair. Rixo wasn't entirely for destruction. He was learning cause and effect and how to change his world. Destroying things was an easy and dramatic way. He'd learn other ways to interact with the world as he grew. He was a curious child. Super cute.

I wasn't new to lockdowns. Working with Moto, our jobs depended on the "Orkain forecast" to decide whether we'd stay inside or tend the gardens. At least Rixo kept me company. He made my heart burst with his energy and emotion. Though it was a double-edged sword today. The lockdown bothered Chelk, but his frayed edges needed rest. He didn't even drink fah which was stimulating like tea.

I secured the string to the other part of the toy with extra knots to protect it from its last fate. Rixo declared a new game where his father dragged the toy behind him while Rixo chased it with—between my translation and context clues—"the whacking stick." He forgot me, and I admired Rixo and Chelk connected in chaotic laughter instead of crisis.

Crisis was not far. The whacking stick took out the cups of rinse water and fah. I had moved them against the wall on the far edge, thinking I'd return to them later and that Rixo couldn't reach them. I was wrong on both counts. A sepia sea ruined my sepia leaves. The deluge washed away the details, soaked the paper, and threatened the floors of two rooms.

Chelk cursed, and Rixo cried.

"It's okay," I said in a soothing voice, unsure who I was comforting.

I used my paper to corral the brown water from falling to the floor, where I worried it would stain.

"You can't do this stuff with kids in the house," he said, mopping up the water that had spilled on the floor on the other side, saying nothing of my painting.

"I'm sorry. I'll clean it up. You help Rixo."

The poor boy had enjoyed the reaction he got from smacking the cup, but now no one was paying him any attention as we dealt with the aftermath. Chelk tossed me a towel before kneeling to speak to Rixo. Lockdowns and parenting were more complicated than I thought. I hadn't meant to create a mess and a scene. Nor was it my fault.

I spent the evening washing the towels we used to clean up my mess and the rest of the laundry. Xavian machines washed and dried in the same machine, much like their showers. I marveled at the efficiency.

Everything needed to be folded and stored. Rixo's little clothes and diapers were adorable. I pulled something stiff from the pile and held it out. Chelk's pants had shriveled and warped. Too big for me and not big enough for him. I hadn't grown up on a farm or ranch wearing leather chaps. Shit. They weren't supposed to go in the machine. I had ruined them. If Chelk knew the phrase "This is why we don't have nice things," he'd repeat it many times today.

"I'm sorry," I started again.

Chelk's face fell. "Those were my favorite."

Of course they were. Ugh.

Rixo cried at full volume most of the evening. I tried but couldn't stand shutting myself in my room. It didn't give me any extra peace to isolate myself. I kept vigil with Chelk.

"I don't know what's wrong with him," Chelk said, at wit's end. Neither of us knew.

"Is he getting sick?" I worried I could give him a human sickness, but I'd been on the planet for half a year now without causing illness.

"Could be the change in routine, as you said." He sighed. "I just want him to be happy."

He didn't want an easier or quieter life for himself. He wanted happiness for his little one. His father bounced him up and paced. His eyes held worry. How much was Chelk carrying?

The end of the day brought exhaustion. The urish was dry, but Chelk needed more sleep than the urish could supply.

"If he goes to sleep, you can have your side of my bed," I offered.

My eyes were heavy, and Rixo whined. I didn't catch his reaction, or if he had heard me. Too shy, I didn't repeat myself.

The bed was cold when I climbed in, but I was thankful for the horizontal position and for the safe shelter. Lockdown had kept us safe. And despite our noise, Chelk assured me that the Orkain couldn't hear us in our hidden home.

Chelk slipped into bed hours later. In my sleepiness, I wished he'd cuddle against me. Would I feel safe in his arms or crushed? He stayed so far away from me. So respectful, and snoring again.

Thankful for his nearness and enveloped in his sleepy, spiced scent, I relished the full, safe, warm bed. Close enough, I fell back asleep.

Chapter Fourteen
Keeping Up

Chelk

It'd been a weakness that let me drop into Layla's bed last night. A mistake that I paid for when painful erections woke me with a start. They were going to get me kicked out of Layla's bed. I stole a glance over the curves of her body. That didn't help. I kicked myself off the bed. Well, I moved to a sitting position before standing slowly. I didn't want to fall over with a horrifying thump when my legs gave way.

In the hallway, the settit's violent violet flash signaled for me to report. I couldn't until I dealt with my cocks. They rubbed mindlessly while I brushed my teeth. I considered a cold shower. I didn't jack off often, not since I was a boy growing into my hormones. It was the stress of the lockdown…or the way she smelled of sweet fruit and sunshine. How would she taste, gently between my teeth? I increased the friction. I'd praise her as I played with the limits of her pleasure. She'd call out my name as I filled her.

Fryyre, my cocks shuddered, my hands gripped the stone bench as three jets squirted toward the shower drain. They milked against each other and spilled a surprising amount. I pulled the heavy, thick strands from my cocks with another shiver of pleasure. Kicked it towards the drain and rinsed me and it, the entire time kicking myself for taking so much time. I didn't have this same sexual tension with Stella. I also didn't sleep in her bed.

But damn, I needed the sleep.

* * *

The moments to myself went unnoticed. The house was still quiet when I called Vjann. Vjann's heavy, thick locks caught in his horns, making him look wild and unkempt. While we were on lockdown, he'd been busy.

"Haellea Zoroso," I greeted him.

"You must report."

He had no time for niceties and assumed I was shirking my duties. Of course not, I was the base. Lian needed me. Kane was the only unnecessary one.

"My kid—" I started.

Vjann grunted. "Take him wherever you need to take him. Wherever that is." He looked off screen, distracted, finished with this conversation.

"Yes, Zoroso," I said and disconnected.

I had permission to move anyone where they'd feel more comfortable. Before plans could formulate, Rixo's bubbly giggling drifted through the room. It was unusual for him to wake cheerfully. He must be getting into trouble. I leaped and ran to his room, expecting his dirty diaper to be smeared somewhere. *If he did that again…*

The door was open. Inside, Layla changed Rixo's diaper, and they giggled together. Interrupting a diaper change was dangerous. I hung back in the hallway, grateful. Stale, cold pee wasn't my favorite. There's worse after his morning meal. Xavians dropped breakfast after the first couple of growth spurts, but humans carried the habit into adulthood. They drank milk from other animals, too. Weird. Stella had told me that one.

Neither of them looked for me. I was ready to take them to Gulshan's, but that wasn't necessary. Did they even need me?

"Hah-zah!" Rixo called for me.

My jealousy evaporated.

"Huh-lay," greeted Layla. Her pronunciation was wrong. It must be difficult with only one tongue.

"Haellea," I said in return, not meaning to correct her.

"Haellea," said Rixo correctly.

"Hay-lay," Layla tried again. Very close.

"Hay-lay," said Rixo.

Mm, I hoped he didn't learn her stilted tongue. Learning English benefited him. English sounds weren't difficult, but there were many rules and exceptions. I wasn't great at the language, but I communicated well enough. And I was learning.

"I talked to Vjann. Lockdown remains in place, but soldiers are being asked to report in."

"I suspected as much. So, you'll have to go. I can take care of Rixo here."

I'm glad it was her suggestion. "You don't have to." I explained the other options.

"No, it's safer for Rixo to stay here. We will be okay by ourselves here. I can manage."

What she said made sense. Truth be told, I didn't want Layla out there either. As much as I hated lockdowns, those who obeyed them stayed alive. I thanked her.

I went over emergency directives and guidelines as I prepared to leave—Gulshan would check in on them. Layla's smile weakened and faded.

"Are you sure you're okay with this?" I asked.

"Yes, I'm just nervous about where you're going…"

I tried to read between her carefully chosen words. Rixo learned quickly, no matter what language you used. Every day he understood more. She feared for my well-being. Why, because she was providing me childcare or because she cared?

"When will you be back?"

"Not sure. I've only been told to report in."

I didn't know how to assuage her worry.

"He won't eat that." I whispered as she prepared food. If Rixo heard me, he'd make it true.

Her bright smile returned. She shrugged. "We'll see."

I hugged Rixo so tight he squealed. I had kept him too long from lining up his toys by whatever today's rule was. A quick glance told me in order of preference. When he escaped, he hugged Layla's legs. I had set off a round of hugs. He understood more than I expected. She patted his head and then lifted her arms to me.

I hesitated. My body stiffened. Rixo watched. Her touch raised the hair on my arms. I carried that buzz until my teammates' violent energies overcame it.

Chapter Fifteen
Surviving

Layla

Tense as he was broad, his arms enveloped me as my knees weakened. The sparkling discs of his eyes spun in sync with the butterflies in my chest. I fit perfectly. That had to mean something, right?

He released me in a daze, forced to steady me by my elbow. *Calm down, girl.* Chelk recovered faster than me. His only reaction was a small cough in his throat. I didn't care if he thought me silly or emotional. Sometimes I felt sparks when others didn't. Besides, there was much at stake. I'd remember his touch.

Another round of hugs. Rixo hugged his father again and then wrapped his arms around my legs as we waved goodbye to Chelk, who left for goodness knows where. I felt a fearful heave in my chest, but I choked it down and squatted to Rixo's height with a big smile on my face.

"What do want to do today?" I asked Rixo.

"Paint!" he shouted, which made my heart soar to a height nearly as high as his father's touch had sent me.

"Do you want to eat breakfast first?" I asked.

"No!" he shouted.

"What do you want to eat?" I tried again.

"No!" he shouted with a big smile on his face.

"Okay, fine, we can paint experiment first, then we eat breakfast, deal?"

"No deal!"

Hm, I needed to think of something else. "What if we experiment with our breakfast foods while we eat them?"

"Deal!"

I tried to use Xavian words whenever possible, but Rixo was learning a lot of English. Not wanting to teach him incorrect Xavian, I defaulted to English often.

We experimented with various breakfast items, introducing them to water, and seeing if they produced paint. Few things worked as well as fah. Other were disastrous, hilarious, and/or smelly. Most things were inert and a disappointment. It deteriorated as Rixo soaked his toys in water and scraped them across the paper.

"Do you think any of these will be good for painting?" I displayed the remaining armful of things he'd given me.

"No!" he shouted, always shouting.

He was right. Wooden blocks and rubber figurines did not 'paint.' I dumped them into his half-full toy box.

The settit's notification above us made me jump, sending my hand to my chest. Cassie's golden-blond hair and tired smile filled the frame.

"It's Cassie!" I told Rixo, answering the device.

She had oily hair, bags under her eyes, and a content smile as she nursed Cash. His pink face wrinkled around the biggest eyes. I'd kept Cassie's pregnancy secret for months before she fell in love with Zade.

They lived in a cave which kept them safe from the Orkain, and they'd covered nearly every hard surface with blankets. She was such a cute, worried mom. She'd relax with time. They were planning for more. Cassie loved Rixo and had so many questions. I'd been jealous when she delivered Cash. Now, a few phone calls later, Rixo ran laps. It wasn't what I expected, but it was fun.

"How is the new guy?" Cassie asked. "I noticed you mostly talk about Rixo."

"Rixo's the only one here. Chelk's training."

"I don't think they're training, Lay. Zade's out there too and he only helps them with explosives."

My heart stopped for a moment. She was right. They didn't need explosives for training. Zade was a miner. He exploded mines and caves.

"What have you heard?" I asked, curious what she might have picked up from her partner.

"They found a cave where lots of Orkain live."

My eyes asked many more questions, but Cassie shrugged her shoulders. A cave—could others be there? The Orkain abducted their victims. They'd killed many of them, but that didn't mean all of them. Was Bonnie alive? Kaytor? Had Chelk survived because Kaytor lived?

She was a stranger to me, but she was family to them. If she returned home, I'd lose mine, Chelk, and Rixo. I was an optimist, but that scared the hell out of me. If it could be taken in an instant, was it mine?

Meanwhile, I played mommy duty. Rixo jumped on the couch and I hovered in rescuing distance. I understood why Cassie had put blankets everywhere for her baby. This one climbed everything. Happiness was fleeting. If Chelk returned needing me, I'd be here.

"What's he like when he is there?" Cassie asked, reading my mind.

"Tired. He takes care of Rixo when he's home, and by the time he gets Rixo in bed, he's falling asleep on the couch. Or…" I trailed.

"Or what?" she asked, her smile growing large at the possibilities.

"No, I let him sleep in my bed because the couch is so small and Rixo wakes up at the slightest noise so he can't sleep in there with him."

"And he doesn't try anything?"

"Nope, he falls asleep before I do. He's almost too respectful. How do you have quality time with Cash there?" Rixo climbed onto and then back off my lap.

"Cash sleeps a lot, fortunately, so we still get time to ourselves. You need a babysitter and date night."

"Are date nights acceptable when there's a war going on?" I expected a lot from a single dad and soldier.

"Rixo could stay with me and Zade for a bit. I want to know what to expect for our next baby."

"Chelk won't want to be away from Rixo long but maybe we can trade time. That way we both get some kid-free nights."

She seemed amenable to that. Cash had drunk his fill. She patted his back as he let out an enormous burp and fell asleep. He slept a lot.

"How is the painting going?"

"I'm running out of paint," I confessed.

"How are you going to survive?" She asked, only half joking. She knew that was my outlet.

"I'm going to figure out how to keep painting. I'll make my own paints."

* * *

After I got off the call with Cassie, I chased Rixo around the house. He was fast on chubby light green legs, lighter colored than his father. Would his skin darken as his horns grew? We ran around in circles until we were both giggling so hard we couldn't breathe. His nose was big and flat, and his smile was infectious. He had eyes like his father's…dark forest green spirals, more alien than the horns or the skin color.

I offered him food, but he wasn't interested in anything that wasn't playing, yelling, and running. More food ended scattered on the ground than in his stomach. Rixo was the sweetest, and I was falling in love. But that wasn't enough. Rotha existed and I tired of being sidelined. Waiting for Chelk made my helpless heart grow fonder. I missed his sour disposition and his critical thinking skills.

Rixo was adorable, but his reasoning was difficult to relate to for an entire day. By evening, Rixo and I annoyed each other. He didn't want to eat any of his dinner and kept asking for ha-zah. I couldn't produce his father, and so he didn't want to have anything to do with me. He wore more food than he ate, and I couldn't catch him to wash him in the sink. I didn't try the shower, afraid he'd run and slip. And then he threw up what bit he had eaten. And all the time, he kept screaming for his father. I gave him water and wondered where his father was.

Trapped in the bedroom, Rixo jumped on the bed and ran laps until he fell asleep half-dressed in the dead center of his father's bed. Kneeling with my arms on the bed, I didn't dare move. I understood why his father slept on the urish. I fell asleep, drool collecting in the crooks of my arm-pillows.

Chapter Sixteen
Orkain Roost

Chelk

Soldier movement during a lockdown was too obvious, so protocol kept me off the trails and in the depths of the jungle. The thick canopy thinned the sunlight passing through, but I kept my senses alert. I didn't want to get wasted by an Orkain before I contributed.

Lian handed me my shield, which he'd picked up from the armory. He offered me tak, a woven packet of fah leaves. His wad rolled around wet in his mouth. The plant stimulated tongues, gums and calmed upset stomachs. It served as a distraction for anxious fellows. I didn't need it.

"Late again," Kane said, ignoring Lian tapping his arm with the tak.

"Yeah," I replied.

Our team was off to a great start.

Vjann commanded our attention, moving soundlessly to the mouth of the cave, eclipsing the light. The cave echoed and amplified his voice.

"Today will be your first test."

More like *today I'm using you as our first test.* Not only the teams, but our strategy was untested. No matter what happened, Vjann (or someone after him) would analyze, improve, or scratch the idea altogether if it wasn't effective.

Lian bounced around like Rixo. I put a heavy hand on his shoulder to ground him. He needed to focus that energy. I was to send him into the air on top of an Orkain double his size. Vjann and others had scouted a cavern that had many Orkain in it.

"They're in a cave with a quick drop-off so we can't go inside and fight. Instead, Zade will collapse the cavern. We've located potential exits. I've assigned your trio the main entrance or one of the exit tunnels."

I shot a stare at Kane. Asshole called me out for being late rather than updating me. He mouthed our answer—entrance.

"Fliers will launch at anyone exiting."

He turned without another word, leading us west.

The shield on my back, Lian to my left, and Kane taking point, we moved through a wetter part of the jungle. Water dripped from the upper leaves of the canopy onto the lower leaves. The jungle's shedding of its most recent downpour sounded like Orkain's wings moving through the tall trees. Everything glistened and caught my eyes, mistaken for movement.

While others took positions, we remained near the hidden entrance with the leaders and Zade. I wasn't familiar with this cave. Zade didn't recognize it either, and began a heated discussion with Vance, pulling him to the side.

I couldn't hear any of it, but it wasn't good news. The buzz in my chest kept the same frequency as Lian's bobbing horns. Lian looked flighty, mumbling something to himself around the tak. The sooner we start, the better for him. The better for all of us. Kane was the only one who kept his cool.

Prince Drex moved toward the pair. Now we'd get started.

Nope, more talking. Still couldn't hear it. I shifted my weight from foot to foot. My quads twinged. I tipped onto my toes to stretch them. I needed to stay limber. A base fallen over with a cramped muscle was useless. Vance stomped to Vjann, his body tense. They spoke in hushed whispers.

Vjann approached. We huddled together for our next command. Finally, the news trickled to us.

"We're aborting the mission. Clean up your tracks here. They can't know we were here."

We asked why, but Vjann didn't answer.

Fryyre. We were here…for nothing? I fought the urge to kick a nearby tree, or Zade—who had second guesses and now we were going home. I wasn't the only angry Xavian trying to ease their energy. Kane marched home without helping to stir up the stamped leaf litter. Lian laughed uncomfortably, coming off the adrenaline. They'd gotten us excited and scared for nothing.

We retreated and separated. On my way home, I considered that stupid waste of time. There were Orkain in there. Were there Xavians, too?

At first, the Orkain wasted our bodies. We lay strewn in pieces, vast distances from original locations. After our numbers dwindled, abductions became standard. We rarely found those bodies. Were they in that cave?

Kaytor had been gone for two years. We weren't rotha mates. I wasn't at risk of dying, but I wanted death. If she had lived in those two years, she would have tried to escape and return to Rixo and me…would have died trying. Still, could I move on with Layla without knowing?

No wonder Vjann remained silent. None of us would have left if we'd known of possible survivors. It was ridiculous to think one of them could be Kaytor, just an excuse to peg myself with guilt for the attraction I felt. The darkness swarmed with my emotions. It was late when I made it to my door, and no one greeted me.

The knot in my chest fell to pieces when I found them in my room. My sweet boy spread across the bed's center with the blankets kicked off, upside down. Layla slept kneeling by the bed, face smashed against the mattress's side. Her soft curls covered her face and the tiniest line of drool.

I had missed them.

Chapter Seventeen
Unpaired

Layla

Fingers grazed my shoulder and brushed the hair from my face. I awoke to fine motor skills, not the slap-handedness of a toddler. Chelk leaned above me. In the middle of his bed lay Rixo, asleep. Even in my drowsiness, I needed no reminder who sudden movements might wake. A night together was at stake.

My knees creaked as he guided me from the room, his eyes having adjusted. How long had he been with us? Somehow, I didn't mind.

He shut the door. I squinted as the living room flooded with light.

Thankfully, Chelk was as I remembered him. Muddy but uninjured. Of all the conflicting feelings, one thought gave peace. *He had returned.* I threw myself into him, jumping to wrap my arms around his neck.

"Whoa," he said, holding me around my torso.

He smelled of pine—woodsy and sharp. Invigorating and enticing, like a secret cabin hidden in the woods.

That buzz remained in my limbs even on solid ground.

"What happened? Did you find the Orkain's home?" I asked, pulling him to the urish.

His brows furrowed. "How do you know about that?"

"Cassie," I said, as if that explained it all.

"You women are impressive." He marveled. "We were going to blow up the cave, but Zade convinced them not to. Maybe Cassie will tell you why."

"Survivors?"

He shrugged. "There is a drop-off inside. You need wings to find out."

I had to ask. It'd been on my mind since Cassie and I had talked. "Is there a chance…Kaytor?"

"No," Chelk barked. His eyes darkened, and their spin slowed. "There's no hope."

"But what about the rotha bond? Could it be that's why you've survived? Because she's not dead?"

"We were not rotha bound. Just partners."

"Oh," I hadn't realized. Goosebumps rippled across my chest. I couldn't pry anymore. His grief and sadness were real, and my apology not enough. "I'm sorry."

"Yeah. I'm going to wash up. It's late. But how was Rixo?"

I shared our day and concerns about how little he ate. Chelk chuckled and expressed having the same fears every day.

"Thank you for caring for him." He got up to leave.

I bounced a leg to get up the nerve. "You can sleep with me…I mean, in the bed with me tonight," I offered, feeling much braver this time, though still fumbling my words.

"Thank you," he replied.

If I were his mate, I'd follow him into the bathroom and help. Instead, I slipped into the cool bed, leaving him room. I chided myself for being silly, thinking Chelk would bring his wife back from the dead. *I must like him.*

The air escaped me as he entered the room. Damn, should I be sleeping with someone I liked? Somehow it felt heavier, and not just his weight changing the incline of the mattress. Measured movements ensured we did not touch. I was cognizant of my body, its curves, his limbs, bulk, and the minimal dark distance between us.

I longed for the comfort and warmth of his heavy limbs. Acting on impulse and want, I fell into the space between us, a small spoon to his thick ladle.

"Is this okay?" I asked.

"Yes." His frame tensed.

"You can put your arm around me." I released him from the *No Touching* rule.

"Okay."

He did no such thing, nor did he pull away or leave.

"Do you want me to move back?"

"No."

He hardened against my ass. The nudge wasn't unfamiliar, but the cast was. Warmth pooled between my legs. I fought a primal, naughty urge to grind against him. Hardening wasn't consent, and he hadn't put his arm around me.

Hard behind me, he fell asleep. On his side, he didn't snore. I found comfort in his expanding chest against me and his breath warming the top of my head.

I reasoned I'd suffocate under his arm. He was much larger. He could overtake me. Even as he slept, that thought thrilled me. Him on top of me, wrists held above me as he licked, kissed, and bit his way across my body. He'd grab my hips, drag me across the bed, drive those behind me *into* me and claim me as his own.

He shifted, and my breath caught. There was no way for him to read my thoughts or know the wetness between my thighs. Unable to touch myself, I nuzzled close. In his sleep, he put his arm around me.

Perhaps in his dreams he put his arm around her, but this was my dream come true.

Chapter Eighteen
Sun to Me

Chelk

My skin tingled where we touched, and I fought to stay still. Layla fit perfectly, asleep in my arms. Her mop of curly hair hid her gorgeous alien coloring. Not interrupting her sleep was an excuse to be close. I didn't want it to end. Unfortunately, my cocks ruined it. She stirred, arching her neck, and gave me a sleepy smile.

"Huh-lay," she said. Giggling, she cleared her throat and tried again. "Haellea."

"Haellea," I mumbled.

She was too damn cute. I untangled from her warmth, making a quick escape. She smiled, eyeing and inflating my erections. They pressed against the thin fabric of my shorts. She bit her lip, adding another perfect curve to every curve in her body. How could she be so perfect? Was she even real? I needed to get out of here. It was time to go.

* * *

Today was a different day. No lockdown. No guard duty. I was free to spend time with Layla and Rixo. And what did Rixo want to do?

"Swim! Swim! Swim!"

He mimicked the arm strokes around the living room.

"Wow, that's fantastic!" said Layla, impressed. She'd been even more impressed when she saw the boy was a fish.

He'd been pushing to swim since Layla arrived, and we hadn't been able to go. Poor guy had been stuck inside houses. I was excited to swim, too. I prepared lunch, though helena berries were plentiful along the way.

Setting off, Rixo alternated between hanging on my back or sitting on my shoulders, constantly on the move despite not touching the ground. I used one arm to support him, and the other to help Layla when needed. I picked helena berries for Rixo. He grabbed at the bushes and pulled handfuls of helena berries, leaves, and twigs from his spot, but I impressed him by providing him the ripest pink helena berries. I shared with Layla as well. To my delight, she started picking them and giving the best ones to Rixo too. I appreciated her kindness and her closeness as she handed Rixo helena berries. She leaned against me, hand on my arm, on her tiptoes to reach. She smelled sweeter than the helena blooms.

Rixo vibrated with excitement. I held on tight to him. When I wasn't much older than him, I'd bound to this watering hole and jump in at full speed. Under the threat of Orkain, I had to teach a more cautious approach. Our entrance and splash could draw attention, but time had benefited this location. The trees had grown older, taller, and the canopy stronger—the clearing wasn't much to spot. And once in the cool water, we were invisible.

I let Rixo slide off my back. His clothes flew off as he bounded away.

"Wait for us!" panicked Layla.

Too late. He swung on a vine toward the water's center. Not yet coordinated to grab his knees into a ball, he dropped smoothly into the water.

"It's all right. He could swim before could walk."

Layla waited with bated breath until he surfaced near us. She sighed with relief and a "good grief." I didn't know what that was. She laughed as he swam with much more grace than his toddler body had on land. He spun and splashed.

I pulled off my linen shirt and stretched, hoping to distract Layla. She was becoming more comfortable with Rixo's swimming skills, or she risked my son's life to gape at my physique. I must admit, soldiering had its benefits over cooking and eating all day. I undid my pants, pushing them over my hips and thighs, revealing lower abdominal muscles. The hungry look in her eyes tempted me to strip further.

She noticed me noticing. Her cheeks turned a rosy pink and her lips pinched tight. Breaking into a grin, I sprinted and jumped into the water. Rixo got caught in my undertow. He swam into my arms, growing heavy as I lifted him from the water and threw him into the air. The splash punctuated his screaming laughter.

Layla shyly undressed on the shore, using her pants as a curtain over a swimsuit she'd brought from Earth. Her buttery thighs peeked from either side, and a kissable sliver of midriff sent my mind reeling until a toddler's head charged into my kidney. In my moment of weakness, he climbed on top of me, sinking me, briefly reminding me of my mortality. I launched him into the air. The splash was much larger than I expected. A little shout came from Layla, who'd ventured in mid-thigh. I splashed water in her direction to hear it again and lighten my soul. Her little fingers spread to shield her face. Giggles erupted and seldom stopped, even underwater.

We spent the entire morning splashing, playing games, and diving for little creatures—one of them named Rixo. When I got hungry, I knew Rixo was due for food, but it was difficult to coax him from the water, especially for something as dull and basic as nourishment. He teased by getting within grabbing distance, just to make his escape via his favorite vine. He swung and splashed countless times in an endless loop.

In time, I pulled in a slippery shriek and Layla shoved a piece of fruit into his hand. He ate it away from us, crouched, ready to make his escape. My little man hated lockdowns too. We needed this more than another piece of fruit. So back into the water he went. Layla splashed with him, and they tried to find the roundest, squarest, and most triangle-shaped rocks. I digested my lunch and basked in the dappled shade. The warm, humid air kept us safe. The afternoon was ours.

Chapter Nineteen
Touch Me

Layla

The swimming hole was a magical place where our days blurred with happiness. Every morning, the trail burst with new blossoms, berries, and reasons to laugh. Sweet-smelling honeysuckle and jasmine filled our late afternoons, where the three of us delayed going home like school kids. Chelk made a simple, delicious dinner, and Rixo entertained us. And each precious day culminated in sleeping beside Chelk but not *with him*.

He didn't put his arm around me or his hand on my hip in his sleep. And if I were honest, I wanted *much more*. He turned me on. Huge, half-dressed, and in my bed…he did nothing. It killed me. Why was he so reserved? How do you politely ask someone to ravish you?

Moto and I weren't like this. He didn't want me. I didn't want him. And we didn't sleep in the same bed. Did this tension and chemistry only exist in my head? Did he not like humans? His cocks did. I grazed his leg with my toe. It'd become my night's ritual—touching—breaking that first barrier between us. If it was respect that kept him from touching me, then I'd make sure he knew he had permission. The cool hardness of his shin wasn't unlike his cool exterior personality. Chelk wasn't born on Earth under our sun and moon, but if he was, I bet he'd be a Cancer.

"Do you have astrology on Xavia?" I asked.

"Uh, what?"

"That the relative position of your planet and sun during your birth influences your personality. Our sun passed through the Sagittarius zodiac when I was born."

"It was raining when I was born. My parents joked that's why I was always in a foul mood," Chelk supplied.

"It rained when I was born too! My mom said I was the sunshine that day." Interesting weather brought two different stories. He resembled a thunderstorm—dark, broody, and powerful. "When is your birthday?"

"In four days," he calculated.

I let out a tiny squeal. Xavians didn't celebrate birthdays like humans, but I was going to change that.

"We don't look to the skies for our personality. Our uniqueness is within—in our zarata, and we find commonality in rotha."

Moto had explained zarata as soul—your being. Rotha confused me.

"How does rotha work?" I asked.

Chelk hesitated. "What do you mean?"

I rolled over but couldn't discern his expression in the dark. "Is it rotha at first sight or is there a take-hold period?"

Chelk tensed at the question. I put my hand on his shoulder, breaking the space between us. He thrummed under my touch, the tension shifting.

"It's not always obvious at first. Rotha marks can show up right away or later in the relationship."

"We have nothing like that on Earth. You're on your own picking relationships."

"I did all right. Was that not the case for you?"

"No, I wasn't so lucky. I didn't find *the one* or even *one*. On Earth, it's shameful to not find someone."

"Shameful? How is it your fault?"

"Like I didn't try hard enough to meet new people, or that something was wrong with me."

"That can't be true. You've traveled across the galaxy to meet new people." He was quick to defend me. "Something is wrong with them."

"And being a virgin doubles the shame."

"What's a virgin?"

Moto had explained to me that virginity didn't hold the same stigma or gender bias shit or religious shit it suffered on Earth. Nobody cared if you entered rotha with zero or dozens of past bedmates. Still, I hadn't felt comfortable telling him until now. "I haven't had sex before."

"Human sex? Me either."

I laughed, my heart lightening.

"I don't know you well yet, Layla, but I see nothing wrong with you and plenty wrong with the humans who tricked you. You're not like them. Is that why you left Earth?"

"Yes, I wanted to meet new people."

"And what do you think of them?"

"Far better than the humans of Earth."

Chelk harrumphed, expressing what a low bar he considered that. "Does that mean you'll stay?"

I assumed he meant on Xavia when humans returned for us. The differences between Xavia and the

United States were obvious. And despite the predators in the skies, I also preferred Xavia. Still, this place wasn't *for* me. "If I can contribute, yes. Xavia is in crisis. You don't need to cater to humans who want to live here, too."

"Xavia's not a peaceful place to live."

"Nothing worth having is easy," I recalled the saying. I preferred Xavia and this family. If only he would let me in more than his bed.

I traced his shin again with my big toe. If human feet disgusted him, I was going about this the wrong way.

"You're always so wise."

I laughed, realizing. "Oh, that's another one of those anonymous sayings."

"Anonymous was wise."

"For sure," I agreed.

Excitement swam in my lower stomach, pushing me along a new line of exploration. We were communicating…talking and touching. Well, I was touching him. Desire rocketed through me at a disastrous frequency. Were we late blooming or not meant to be? I wasn't sure if I cared. Rotha, relationships, staying-or-going was for the future. The sexy gentleman was right here. Right now.

I grazed the back of his shoulder and neck with my fingers. His corded muscles rippled under my touch. Was it intentional or something I sparked? More than anything, I wanted his caress.

I guided his huge, heavy paw to my much smaller shoulder. His finger pads traced my shoulder blades and up my neck, mimicking my exploration of him. The heel of his hand eclipsing the hollow of my collarbone. He could crush me, but I felt like the dangerous one. My body burned with his touch. Wanting crashed inside me, pushing me toward him.

A wave of adrenaline preceded his lips crushing mine. Saying time stopped was cliché, but it slowed. I was a high-frequency being, impatient, often frantic. Chelk acted with careful consideration. His moments and movements dragged between us, lingering. I savored as he did. His arm pulled me into him. His heavy leg pinned mine against each other, sweetening the ache building between them. Time dragged, like his tongues. I gasped when our lips parted and my soul returned to my body.

I snuggled as close as I dared. With his hand on my hip, my head buzzed for a long time before I found sleep.

* * *

The rain pounding above nearly drowned the noise of the shower. Alone, I moved into his still-warm spot. He kissed me last night. We were going somewhere. This was happening.

My fingers found their way to my mound, petting my hair, drawing lazy circles around my clit. I buzzed with unreleased sexual tension and slick came fast. Would I have enough time?

I flipped over onto my belly to increase the pressure. I imagined him climbing on top of me. He'd hold my wrists held above my head as he licked, kissed, and bit his way across my back and ass. He would grab me by my hips, drag me across the bed, drive one of his cocks into me, and claim me as his own. It was a pleasant fantasy.

I was running out of time. The shower had stopped, and the dryer had started. I became more furious with my touch. My fingers wound around and pulled on my swollen clit. The door scraped across the floor, and his shadow appeared from the hallway.

Shit! He was going to walk in and catch me. I drew quiet. My breath tore heavy at my chest and throat. My fingers kept smooth and silent movement. I was so damn close. He made me so damn close. My orgasm clawed at my body to escape, turned on by being found.

His shadow didn't move. He didn't enter. Would he stay and listen to me?

The heel of my hand ground into my clit. I fought to stay quiet. I couldn't help it. The orgasm flooded over me, a gasp that brought no oxygen. Warm juices trickled from my cunt clenching on nothing. I gritted my teeth and saw no shadow.

I was alone. He didn't want to come play. Wasn't even interested in hearing me finish.

Fuck. The relief and endorphins only clarified my mistakes. Was he not attracted to me? Was he just humoring me? The same embarrassment of showing my ass on the first day returned. I cleaned up and got ready for an awkward morning. While I read humans well, Chelk was a mystery.

He was in the bathroom again, avoiding me. Did he plan to stay the entire morning in there? I heated the kettle and pulled out a few painting supplies, needing the therapy of both. I had no plan for the blank page, but layers of paint took the shape of the swimming hole and its surrounding boulders.

"That's the jumping rock." Chelk said from behind.

I dropped my brush, reddening, but happy he recognized it. Rixo had jumped from it countless times.

Chelk dropped spaulders on the chair opposite me. He wore his chaps.

"We can't go today. I've got to meet with Kane and Lian," he said.

"Practice? In that downpour?"

"As far as I know. You've got your own ways."

I had heard nothing.

"Rixo and I will stay here?" I asked.

"If you're okay with that."

I felt plenty comfortable with Rixo, and I didn't want to wake him for the trip to Gulshan's.

"Yeah, for sure."

"Thank you. Is there anything you need?"

I leaned toward him. Was a kiss a *need?* No, I shook my head.

He paused, taking his spaulders. "I'll go then."

He didn't brush my elbow or even pat me on the shoulder.

Nope. I definitely messed something up.

The click of the exterior door triggered the scream of Rixo. If Chelk heard it, he didn't return. I hurried to Rixo, not looking forward to telling him the news.

I fed Rixo breakfast, then washed breakfast off him. We played on the bed, and surprisingly, after one hundred back rubs, he slumped over and fell asleep for a rare nap. I expected him to squeal and stop me from leaving, but he didn't.

I put away toys Rixo might not immediately pull back out. Truly, I was procrastinating. I'd come up with this great idea to call Stella and ask about her time with Chelk. Now I had the opportunity. She'd moved in with his commanding officer, Vjann. Awkward, right? I didn't want to poke something that might be painful, but I was eager for some insight. With a quick swipe of my finger and a grit of my teeth, I called.

Stella answered right away. Her hair was a glossy jet black—darker than my mousy brown—long and straight.

"Vjann is in the field. How can—oh, hi, you're Layla, right?" Stella dropped her receptionist demeanor. She had pristine olive-tan skin, and her features were sharp but not harsh. She was gorgeous.

"I am," I said, cheerily. She had a ridiculous glow to her set off by her dark hair and—what were those along her hairline? "Are those rotha marks?"

She nodded, pulling back the wispy baby hairs from her face to reveal the darkening lines, like black ink tattoos. They complimented her hair.

If it hadn't been the fact that they were rotha-bound, destined, perfect for each other—No, I could still see how Chelk might feel crappy about it.

"I wanted to ask about Chelk—" I started.

"He's a grumpy asshole, isn't he?" Stella raised her eyebrows, ready to gossip.

I laughed. It was difficult to disagree with her. She was quick.

I told her how things were here.

Stella's eyes narrowed. "You don't have to let him sleep in your bed. That couch is more private than he ever had in soldier housing. As a host, they gave him that house you're living in."

He lived with Gulshan and the other soldiers with built-in childcare. Private housing was a major benefit, even if the accommodations were small.

She continued. "Switching Day was a formality. I wasn't living there by that time, just my stuff. Maybe he needs you to keep the house or to take care of his kid."

"I like Rixo," I defended.

She shrugged. "He couldn't even talk when I moved in. He didn't have a personality yet."

"Did Chelk cook dinners for you?"

"Didn't have time."

Whatever Chelk and I were doing—was different. Was opening his life to new opportunities? Was it because he thought differently *of me?* We weren't rotha, but we could be something like it.

"Where is the booger?" she asked.

"He's sleeping."

"That's unusual."

"Tell me about it. That kid is a constant motor."

"And the screaming…"

"I'm not a fan of the screaming either," I admitted. "Thanks for talking with me."

With Rixo asleep and Chelk still out, I worked on the painting for Chelk. Chelk didn't appreciate my artwork, but I had little else to give him. Xavians didn't celebrate every birthday, even fewer since the invasion. I loved birthdays. I wouldn't let Chelk's day pass without honoring him. Focusing on the positive was even more important with so much shit happening. Lean toward positivity and the universe will lean that way too.

I struggled to give Chelk something for his birthday because I lived in his house and everything here was already his. Gulshan had remade Chelk's favorite chaps, but we hadn't been over there. I had to make-do, which was unfortunate, but I was still determined to make sure that Chelk had a good day. We needed to celebrate with the people that we loved. We needed more birthdays.

I painted few portraits, but I thought Chelk would like one of himself and Rixo, memorializing this age. I used my cool hues, blues and greens. Unfinished paintings are obvious, but the end-point isn't always so evident. A lot could be gone over, shaded, re-attempted, or made worse. When I ran out of my primary color, I called it finished. It wasn't perfect—Chelk's chin gave me pause—but I was done.

Xavians didn't use wrapping paper. Gifts came hidden in sturdy containers. I intended to use some of Gulshan's scrap fabric to wrap my present. Instead, I searched my closet. Every guest received plenty of clothes of various sizes—some wearable and some not. I picked a print I wouldn't wear and cut out a cloth gift bag, setting the rest aside to be used as rags. I had another gift I wanted to give him, but I couldn't wrap up myself yet.

Chapter Twenty
The Cavern

Chelk

I checked the drainage around the house before setting out. Orkain couldn't fly in this hard rain, and neither could Lian. I didn't understand the point of training unless it was to practice *obedience*. I ran, matching the pace of the rain. I was late, and I needed to shift my blood. Recalling her uneven breath sent me reeling. Needing relief again was desperate and annoying.

Our meeting place was closest to my house, but I wasn't even third to arrive—I was fourth. Kane leaned on the dark, pitted volcanic rock with a scowl. Vjann's face and braid were tight, pulled back. He wasn't here to supervise a practice.

"Back to the cliff," Vjann said.

I grunted my apology and confirmation. Kane and Vjann led the way, leaving me to tend to Lian.

"I've been saying we needed to go back. We should never have retreated."

"It's given us time to prepare new tactics," I reminded him.

"I don't need to train anymore. I'm ready." He puffed his chest, trampling pink moss. His words dripped with a dangerous anger.

I doubted we were attacking in such a small number. We were likely on an information-gathering mission. Vjann led us around the other side of the cliff and even Lian quieted as he navigated the treacherous climb.

When we reached the top, Vjann directed us to move the rock. "See where the water is flowing between these rocks? Zade believes there's another way into the cave. It's been blocked."

We worked under the guise of the storm. The rock layer changed, revealing the glossier stone in slabs. The potential entrance was a tight fit, and Lian volunteered to go alone, but none of us wanted our youngest going alone. Even Kane agreed, and that man was never on my side.

We worked to reach a larger tunnel. The air was stale despite the steady dripping of water. The light from our entrance was not the only one. Someone had hung glow plants. Did they produce enough heat for the Orkain to use, or were others here?

"What the—?" cried a human woman, coming around the corner.

Scared, she turned to run back. Lian moved the quickest, grabbing her and covering her mouth. She squealed under his hand. I had never seen Layla's eyes so wide and frightened.

"It's okay." I whispered. "We're here to rescue you. Are there any more? Any without wings?"

She shook her head. Her mouth still covered.

"To Heljin," Vjann said to Lian and me.

"Bonnie, we're taking you to the doctor." I told her. Her eyes widened—the centers dark, ringed with a sliver of blue. Her hair was unruly like Layla's, though much lighter in color.

She still fought us, and Lian still kept his hand tight over her mouth. "Don't block her nose and be gentle with her," I said as he lifted her parallel to him.

Kane and Vjann crept deeper into the tunnel. There were no others besides her? Kaytor had been gone for two years. I hadn't expected Bonnie to survive a fraction as long. Xavians hadn't been spared. Once out of the tunnel and into the jungle, Bonnie didn't need to be carried, but she didn't follow willingly either.

"No one else without wings is in there?" I asked again.

"Just me and them. How do you speak English?"

Lian interrupted. "We learned for you."

"How many of them are there?"

"I don't know."

"You've lived with them for six months and don't know?"

"That's how long it's been? Wow! No, we joined them recently. A sleep or two?" I held my shield over her head to protect her from the rain. She had on the remnants of silver arrival suits.

"How many in the old place?"

"Just one."

We arrived at Heljin's. He escorted her into his examination room without a single word to us.

We'd saved Bonnie.

* * *

I didn't realize I held my breath, but each one became easier as I walked home. Recalling Layla's painting of the swimming hole, I picked helena berries for her. She could use them in her painting experiments.

The silent darkness in my home unsettled me. Avoiding piles of toys, I dropped the berries on the table before crossing to the closed bedroom door. Inside, my eyes searched and settled on the sweet shapes that were Layla and Rixo sleeping. Too amped to join them, I showered.

My stomach growled as the dryer started. I put on my underpants, kicked the rest into the corner, and headed for the kitchen.

To my surprise, the light was on, and Layla stirred something on the stove. Her sleep clothes hung off her curves, and her legs were bare. I sidled up beside her to see what was in the pot. I caught her scent first, a heady sweetness. My cocks twitched their reception.

"Was it a training drill? You were out so late."

She didn't know. I could lie, give us one night without so much complication, like the simple broth she heated.

I took a deep breath. "Really, it was."

I flexed my quad muscles, trying to decrease blood flow from the inappropriate dinner guests as I poured us two glasses of fage. She tilted her glass toward mine. I didn't like fah, but I liked fage. They came from the same plant, but their preparation and serving styles were different.

"A toast to your return," she said.

She tapped our glasses together, and we both took a sip. I knew nothing about toast.

I set my glass down by a swath of familiar pink and purple fabric. She never liked that dress as much as I did. The house vomited keepsakes and memories with each moon's cycle.

In my hands, I almost felt her strong hips underneath. It smelled of her, and the paint behind it. Layla had cut the dress and tied it around the painting.

"What is this?" I asked about the odd display.

"It's a gift for you. Happy birthday!"

I sank into the urish. She used the dress to cover the gift—strange. My thumb traced the flower in the fabric. The warm flesh of my past love no longer supported it. My love changed shape. She was in Rixo's sheepish grin, the wrinkles in his forehead when he was mad, and in his distaste for clover.

"Are you going to open it?"

Something inside me shifted. I tore my eyes from the present and the past, blinked away tears.

"That's kind of you to give me a gift. I should have told you it's not a special year."

She laughed, a bright, cheerful laugh. Rixo echoed her cadence.

"When are the special years? Gulshan tried to explain you don't celebrate every year."

I often tried to bridge the gap for her, like she often did between Rixo's toddler translations and the language barrier for her and Gulshan was wider than hers and mine. Layla adapted well to Xavian life, but measurements confused her. Revolutions around our sun were much quicker than Earth's.

"In forty-two rainy seasons, I'll be…"

"Oh no, just open it now!" She laughed.

For our culture, Layla had traveled young and far. She called her earlier life boring, as if it had been long.

Now she celebrated my what? One hundred and fifty-eighth rain. Fantastic. With what?

"Where did you get an Earth canvas?" I asked, surprised. I thought she had used them all. We didn't have canvas as made on Earth.

"It isn't. Gulshan made this for me! It's layers of his thinnest linen stretched over a wooden frame. This was the prototype, but it turned out fantastic."

Rixo sat on my shoulders, laughing and smiling. She'd been so busy getting these "Earth" things that she wanted. Part of me wanted her to do Xavian things, but she'd been doing it for me. When had she even painted this?

Now I understood its value over mere photograph evidence. She depicted her care, Rixo's joy. The pleased look on my face mirrored mine. I wished she'd painted herself beside us. She should be by my side, holding my arm, looking up at Rixo. She'd have the same sunshine that Rixo had.

"This is amazing. I don't have English words for it. 'Thank you' doesn't seem sufficient."

"I'm glad you like it," she beamed.

I liked it; I liked her more. *How to tell her?*

"How was Rixo today?"

"He missed you. Tried to convince me to take him swimming."

"In the rain?"

She shook her head. "No way. Too much could happen out there. How would I get help?"

I hated that it wasn't safe enough for Layla and Rixo to play outdoors.

I eyed the broth. "Thank you for the broth, but I think I want something hearty. Do you want something? How about if I cook for you?"

"You don't have to do that."

I wasn't asking. I pulled out more ingredients. Pants be damned. I was going to cook a lot of food. If Layla had concerns, she didn't speak them.

I chopped vegetables into the most perfect, tiniest squares, relishing the knife's sharpness. The squares got tinier and more perfect. This wasn't the perfect way to cope with it, but it let me burn off my energy. And it didn't include pinning the human woman to the wall and fucking her into oblivion with my cocks in her pretty holes.

"Are those helena berries for him?"

"No, they're for you. I thought you'd need them for the helena bushes you were painting this morning."

"Really?" Her face lit up with delight. She hurried to hide them in her room, away from Rixo's smashing tendencies.

Her laughter stirred me. In my favorite ceramic wok, I heated plant oil, infusing it with spices. The aromatics swirled with the thoughts in my head. As Layla's first, I aspired to be nothing less than perfect. She deserved more than a desperate, needy fuck. I needed to seduce her with a fine touch, a fine dinner, and another glass of fage. Like cooking, rushed preparation was not enjoyable. We needed time.

Layla sat on the counter, away from the heat, humming a song. I didn't know it. She told me stories of Rixo, her toothy grin prefacing each thought. The vegetables seared, flavoring the air and whetting my appetite.

I served her in my underclothes. My cocks settled, half-full, unneeded. At least she'd be certain that I was large enough. From the other soldiers, I understood human female anatomy to be much simpler than

Xavian anatomy. Focus on the clitoris and the G-spot behind it. The soldiers didn't understand seduction, though.

Tension strummed through dinner. Partway through the clean-up, Layla's fingers brushed my forearm.

"Give me a few minutes before coming to bed," she said before disappearing into her bedroom.

I scrubbed the pan with new earnestness. Was she touching herself so she could sleep in peace? I wanted to help. My cocks grew restless in my shorts.

After waiting as long as I could, I cracked open her door and paused.

"Come in," she whispered.

My face misfired, mouth falling open as I swallowed. Layla perched on the bed in tiny shorts with a high waist, bare legs crossed. She'd tied the rest of the flower dress as ribbons around her breasts. Luscious pale skin peeked from behind strips. An enormous bow stood center. She had wrapped herself up as a present.

"Wow," I managed, closing the door behind me.

"Come open your present." She giggled. "If I move, it'll fall down."

I didn't mind. I tried to wipe the stupid grin from my face before slowly lowering my weight onto the bed. The fabric shifted. She wasn't lying about its precarious positioning. I cautioned a hand forward.

"Oh no. I think you should open your present without your hands." She said it in a gentle song voice she used with Rixo.

"What should I use?"

"That's up to you." Her words dripped with possibilities. If not for my underpants, my cocks would have volunteered.

Nervous and greedy, I scooted closer. I breathed cool on her neck and admired from that angle. "You are beautiful, wrapped up for me."

Her cheek twitched as she smiled through her sexy, bitten lip. Lowering my face to her chest, I could put the ribbon between my lips or teeth and pull. Instead, I tilted my chin and grazed her breast with the edge of my horn. Her breath hitched with a delightful bounce of her tits. I couldn't stop myself from tasting the prickling goosebumps on her skin. Her breath hitched again. I caught a strip with my horn. The fabric loosened in places and tugged deliciously elsewhere.

With my face between my gifts, I unwrapped them with my tongues. She hummed and giggled. I kissed her soft skin, kissed around her pinkish-brown nipple, and pulled her into my mouth with my tongues. Her breasts were delectable, and the encouraging sounds she emitted were just as sweet. I massaged and licked. My free hand played on her clothed hips. I ran kisses up her curves, her collarbone, her neck.

I kissed her deeply, then pulled away to admire my gift once more. The ribbons had fallen to her waist.

"Do you like them?"

I cursed and dived in again, sweeping her curly hair out of my way. I set out to show my appreciation. She giggled and pulled the ribbons from around her waist. I wished they were around her breasts again. Before I could voice that, she tied my wrists loosely behind my back.

"I told you not to use your hands," she whispered.

She rose to her knees, put her forearms on my shoulders, and leaned forward. I wasn't sorry for my punishment.

Her breasts grazed my face, lips, and tongues. I was hard, trying to bust out of my underpants. She brushed a hand over them before saddling me with those little shorts. I nearly lost it as she grazed against me.

Her breasts in my face again, I obliged her, thankful for the distraction. While I could escape, giving her control was fun. I'd give her anything…significant birthday or not. She was divine.

And turned on. She laid me back, my hands flat beneath me. Her heated core dragged across my abs as she wiggled up my bare stomach in damp shorts. On my cocks, I would have come in one foul stroke. She pressed her breasts onto my lapping tongues. Our physical differences turned her on… my multiple tongues (and cocks), my horns, my thick muscles. I got it. I liked her softness, her round curves upon my hardness. Fryyre, I wanted to touch her all over, but the limits of the binds left it as fiery heat in my chest. She liked playing with me, teasing me. She'd look stunning perched on my cocks. A groan escaped her as she ground on my chest.

"I heard you the other morning," I confessed.

"What did you hear?" she smiled lopsidedly, her blunt pink tongue caught between white teeth.

"I heard you moving in the bed…touching yourself."

"Would you like to watch?" she asked, cutting her eyes at me.

"Yes, please," I breathed.

She slid her hand over her stomach, past her navel. Her fingers played with the hem of her panties. I held my breath and even my cocks paid their respects with stillness as I greedily watched her rub inside her panties.

I craned to watch, so she backed up against my cocks. My cocks worked between her legs, rolling underneath her. Lubricated, they played against each other, her ass cheeks, and her clit.

A sweet whine from her lips accompanied her climax. I have considerable control, but when she came undone, I did too, releasing from more than one cock. Losing sense of myself, all I knew was that I needed to clean myself.

She climbed off me with a sheepish expression, the fog clearing from her eyes. I could sense she was retreating. I sat up and she untied my bonds.

"That was a fantastic birthday," I said sincerely. "Thank you."

Her smile brightened. My naughty woman enjoyed taking control in sex. I would encourage it when we connected and praise it in her shy moments. She curled up next to me, satisfied. I pulled her close, loving her sweet finished scent.

Chapter Twenty-One
Sickening

Layla

In the morning, my bladder forced me to untangle from Chelk's sleeping mass. While nothing had gone according to plan, the night had been mostly a success. If I hadn't tied his hands, we might have touched more.

I checked on Rixo. He'd kicked off his blankets but was motionless. Moving to replace one, the heat he radiated shocked me. His forehead was blazing hot under my palm. He wriggled listlessly, eyes scrunched shut.

I picked him up and called his name. He didn't respond or hold up his head.

I raced into the bedroom for Chelk.

"Rixo, he's hot. He's so hot. He's not waking up."

Chelk woke with a start—upright with a hot babe in his arms. He patted his ruddy-green cheeks. His lips and baby-fat cheeks squirmed when I pinched his cheeks and foot. Otherwise, he didn't cry out or speak to us.

"Run a cool bath, and I'll call the doctor."

He was too hot. We needed to lower his temperature. While the water was running, I dressed and hastily scooped my strips of debauchery from the ground. Was Rixo sick while I humped his dad?

I tried to remember the last things Rixo had eaten. He had a reactive stomach and vomited often, but he didn't seem in distress. Did his bad days outnumber his good days? Was he gaining weight or losing weight?

"The bath—as cold as you need to rouse him—" the doctor started in English when I approached. "But he needs to come see me."

"What is wrong with him?"

"I can't know from here." He turned to Chelk, "Did you have contact with your son last night? The human or Orkain—"

"No, I didn't," he interrupted. "Showered, too."

That wasn't a training drill in the rain.

"Get his fever down and bring him here. Be careful. The Orkain are active."

"Thank you, Heljin. Haellea."

"Haellea."

They disconnected. We moved to the bathing room, plunging our little fish into the chilly water. He coughed, his body shaking with more movement than I'd seen this morning.

"Vjann took our team to a blocked cavern exit. We found Bonnie. She's alive and at Heljin's."

I soaked my hands in the cold water.

"I wanted one night for us," he said, though he eyed his son.

"Was there anyone else?"

"She says no one besides Orkain. You can speak with her through the settit."

Poor woman. Last night, I would have demanded to go. Chelk wanted *one night for us.*

"No, I'm going with you and Rixo. And Bonnie needs someone. So, let's come up with a plan."

He hesitated. "We'll see."

* * *

The plan wasn't great. Chelk sighted an Orkain perched outside our home, waiting for us. He would lead it away so Rixo and I could leave without being followed. Chelk offered a fabric carrier. Silently, he adjusted it from the shape of his partner and babe to that of me and his sick toddler.

With extra blades tucked into his vest, Chelk slipped out and caught the eye of the Orkain. It darted from tree to tree, stalking its prey. Fear burned in my chest. With Rixo constricting my ribcage and breath, I started in the opposite direction.

Behind me, the Orkain screeched. Had it lost interest in Chelk? It careened, clipping its wing on the bramble set for them. I sprinted deep into the jungle, hugging Rixo to me. My sense of direction was the only thing worse than this idea.

I lost the Orkain, but I lost myself, too. Where was I? *Don't panic.*

Fuck. Fuck. Fuck. Rixo stirred against my pounding heart. My head darted in every direction. This sucked. I had to calm myself for Rixo's sake. For my sake.

"It's okay, Rixo. Lala is here." I cooed. I stopped and tried to get my bearings.

The trees looked the same, but what was different? This land was flat. I needed to be going uphill.

Taking a deep breath, I backtracked to find something familiar. I should've picked Girl Scouts over Pep Club. They would have taught me to navigate. It wouldn't hurt for the Xavians to put up signs, either. My stomach did somersaults.

Here. This tree, I recognized. I was off course, but on a path I knew. I hurried, then turned around to hurry the other way. At least I was no longer lost…

* * *

When I reached the cave, I found it empty. I was late for our meeting. He must have gone looking for me. I tapped my foot in impatience. I'd gotten lost once. Could I find my way to Heljin's by myself? No… but I could get to Gulshan. I could get directions from there. Rixo needed medical attention. We couldn't wait here. I stacked five rocks to signal we'd been here, then took the path to Gulshan's.

Rixo stopped fighting. I worried when he stirred, and worried when he stilled. I was terrified I'd reach Gulshan's with a suffocated babe, and too terrified to check.

Gulshan jerked open the door, stunned to see me and Rixo alone.

"Where is Chelk?"

"We got separated. Rixo is sick. I need to take him to Heljin."

"Come in," he pulled at me.

I shook my head, panicked he'd make me stay. Rixo burned.

He conceded. "Heljin—take this path, left at the waterfall of tree roots." He gestured to help my understanding.

"If you see Chelk…"

"I will let him know."

I recognized the "tree root waterfall" Gulshan described. A tree had toppled, and its roots grew downward. I took the left and ran. Heljin's place was easier to spot than others. The path had become worn.

At our destination, I didn't want to give up Rixo. Heljin reached for him, and I bowed away. Fear raced through me.

"I have medicine for him. Let me help," he soothed.

We slowly unwrapped Rixo from my sweaty body. Heljin examined him and gave him the medication he had prepared.

"That was it?" I asked, shivering.

He provided me with a blanket.

"Yes, you did well, Layla. I'll give him another dose, and you'll stay here overnight. We're on lockdown. Where is his father?"

I explained how our plan went awry. I assumed Chelk had made it to the cave, but what if he hadn't?

His physician's eyes turned to me. "Any injuries sustained on your journey?" he asked.

"Nothing a cup of fah can't fix."

He gave me a comforting pat on my shoulder. "Rixo's a tough baby. Difficult birth. Difficult baby. Are you experiencing any signs of rotha, pains, marks?"

"My chest hurt today, but I think that was from the running."

I didn't want to replace Kaytor, especially when I felt alien here. Rotha mates had honing abilities for their mates. We hadn't experienced that in the jungle.

"There's still time. Rotha is a strange and unknown thing for humans. Most of your books are about men.

Why no studies for half of your species?" He shook his head. "As long as no other patients arrive, you can use these beds."

"Thank you. Do you have anyone training under you?" I asked. The invasion created gaps in generations and knowledge.

"Two, but I'd welcome more, especially a human. Do you have any prior knowledge?"

I shook my head. It interested me, and I wanted to help. I just didn't know how.

"No one else does either," he said encouragingly.

I thanked Heljin. "May I meet Bonnie?" I asked.

* * *

Bonnie kept her door shut. She hardly peeped her consent. However, Heljin seemed accustomed to her mousy volume and swung the door wide open.

Bonnie tucked away the familiar silver suit behind her. Her frizzy blond hair framed a round face, filled with giant pools of blue eyes. They widened impossibly larger when they saw me.

"Hi, I'm Layla. I was on the ship with you."

"I wasn't sure if y'all survived," she said with a Southern twang.

"We didn't think you did either. No, we're all alive."

She wore oversized clothes that belonged to Heljin. Poor thing didn't have clothes, her belongings, and she was alone.

"What's going to happen to me?" she asked. "Heljin said I would move in with a male Xavian. I told him *no.*"

"It's not bad. I lived with Moto, a farmer. Now I'm with a warrior and his son. There are no Xavian females to host."

"Because of the—what do you call them?"

"The Orkain. What did you call them?"

"Demon," she mumbled.

I couldn't fathom what she'd been through.

"You're safe now."

Bonnie stared at her lap, shaking her head.

Chapter Twenty-Two
Chase

Chelk

Slipping past the Orkain had taken too much time. When I reached the cave, Layla had come and gone. I ran to Heljin's home and hoped they were there.

"Oh, good. You're here." Heljin said, when I arrived.

"Rixo? Layla?"

Pain ripped through my chest, making it difficult to think.

"Yes, they are here. Have been. I treated Rixo for the infection. He's sleeping heavily, recovering."

Heljin had a large dwelling like Gulshan's, but the rooms were for patients, not soldiers. I wasn't fond of either place.

He led me into an austere room with a simple futon bed and a crib. My heart raced, transported years ago, approaching the same crib. He was larger, stronger. I pulled his long, soft hair behind his ear. He was no longer fire-hot. His chest rose and fell with his breath as I settled my own.

"He'll be okay," said Layla, coming from another room. Beside Xavian furniture, she looked small, too.

"Are you okay?" she asked.

I shook off the grief and worry. "It took longer than I expected to slip away from that Orkain, but I'm fine. Why did you go on without me?"

So many things could have gone wrong, but she'd gotten my son to medical care. How mad could I be?

"I thought you'd already been there and left. Rixo was sick, so I made a choice."

"Thank you for getting him here." I held and kissed her.

I remained rooted next to Rixo for most of the morning, but by afternoon, I investigated Heljin's kitchen. Ingredients were lacking, and lockdown prevented foraging. Still, I was determined to cook everyone a good meal as a thank-you. After I became accustomed to Heljin's kitchen and ingredients, I set to task.

Heljin and Bonnie enjoyed the multi-course meal late into the evening with Layla and me. Layla boasted all evenings were this delicious at our house. She wasn't wrong. Heljin thanked me over and over for the meal. I don't think he'd eaten like that since the public house was open. I was the exception. I'd forgotten how far our culinary standards had sunk since the Orkain invasion. A good meal brought joy. Even Bonnie lightened, becoming more comfortable with us over the course of dinner.

Layla helped me clean up the kitchen, and Heljin and Bonnie retired for the evening. I helped Layla translate a medical textbook provided by Heljin, encouraging Layla's interest. The sophisticated text challenged my English. We settled for the basics, and

I quizzed her on Xavian anatomy. She touched me where I directed. Soon it devolved into touching each other.

She picked up my hand with hers and mangled the Xavian word. "Let's find another room." She pulled me from the table and into the hall.

She skipped the first room with Rixo. The second room's doorknob didn't budge, locked. She moved to the next room, trying to find an open spare room.

The locked rooms blocked us. Never discouraged, Layla patted back into the main living area. She swiped a set of keys from the desk and fisted them into the air, beaming triumphantly. Layla was a naughty, persistent woman.

"We don't have to do this," I tried as she tried multiple keys.

While I wasn't too keen on the setting, Layla's mood never dampened. It was contagious, arousing. Rotha be damned, I didn't want to deny her desires.

"Scared? Heljin could be right behind this door." She winked at me.

"Go ahead," I said as if she needed my encouragement.

She unlocked the door, swinging it open. The room had the same austere furniture, though no crib. Death clung to it—all the patients, comrades, and friends lost. Layla disappeared, too. Had she changed her mind?

No, she came nearly skipping back, having returned the keys.

"I didn't want to forget," she said. She leaned against the closed door. "We have more anatomy to learn."

She straddled me on the bed, grinding on me. I churned beneath her.

"Touch me," she requested.

"Show me how."

My hand stretched her waistband low to find delightful curls. My thumb toured parallel to heated wetness, settling on hooded flesh. Moving in slow, gentle circles, guided by Layla's whimpers, I worked her.

Her cheeks flushed. I maneuvered lowered, to drag more slickness to her clit. She was wetter than I expected.

"I love this," I whispered into her ear, an excuse to get closer to her moans.

I timed my kisses and thumb. My cocks pressed against her, wanting friction. She rocked against me and crushed me into a kiss. Her thighs clenched, then everything relaxed. Her release.

I wanted it again.

* * *

The next morning, Rixo had enough strength to sit up and greet me. He scrunched my face with his chubby fingers and slapped my horns. He was healthy enough to return home, but we had to get past the Orkain. They'd remained active, likely looking for Bonnie. With no Orkain sighted, we took our opportunity. I wrapped Rixo tight against me, which angered him. I helped Layla along the quickest route home. We would not split up again. That panic had been unbearable.

A hundred meters from home, I spotted the dark, winged creature. I pushed Layla off the trail and deeper into the brush.

"What's going on?"

She hadn't seen it.

I pointed it out as it made another pass. "It's circling…waiting."

Still, we could get home.

We stumbled through the leaf litter. Layla's eyes were wide, and slipped often.

Rixo wailed in my ear. I cooed futilely. I couldn't hear the Orkain over him. We were almost home with one more clearing to cross.

"I'm going to carry you."

With Rixo sandwiched between us, I scooped up Layla, her legs hugging my waist. I might not have been able to run any faster carrying Layla than if she ran alongside, but now we were inseparable. Adrenaline pumped through my sprinting legs.

"Does it see us?" I asked Layla who had a view over my shoulder. She'd know if we were in trouble.

"No, it's going the other way. *Hurry.*"

Under the door's outcropping, I set Layla down to unlock the door. I hastily unwrapped Rixo from me, passing him over the threshold before closing the door between us. Layla and Rixo shouted from the other side, angry but safe, while I searched the skies and tree-line. The Orkain was nowhere to be found. Where had it gone?

Inside, I pushed the urish in front of the door. Layla held Rixo tightly. He fought her, throwing fists and yelling. He needed to run. We had built up stress, and he needed to release his.

"Let him go," I said.

Her eyes flashed with terror, though her grip loosened. Rixo slipped away, and running circles. She buried her head between my arm and chest until her breathing slowed.

"It's okay. We're safe in here. It's okay," I soothed her. I gave her what she wanted to give Rixo. I stumbled over the English, and partway through gave up, speaking words of safety and love in Xavian. She nearly disappeared in the safety wrap of my arms. I kissed the top of her little head where her hair parted. In Xavian, I apologized if we were rotha mates. She wasn't safe on my planet.

It took a moment to realize I was the one shaking, and not Layla anymore. She shook her head free from my giant embrace and focused her worry on me.

"I'm sorry." I said, sniffing. She needed strength.

"Don't be sorry," she said. "Thank you for getting me to safety."

"I'm sorry." I couldn't protect Layla.

"It's not your fault. The Orkain is an evil. It's not your fault," she repeated firmly.

Intellectually, I understood I wasn't responsible for the Orkain. But it was my duty to protect my family, and I failed at it.

Chapter Twenty-Three
Preparation

Layla

Heljin contacted us on the settit.

"Bonnie is gone. Is she with you?" He asked.

No, we had no idea. Was that why the Orkain didn't pursue us? Was it pursuing Bonnie?

"Why did she leave?" I asked.

"She went back to the Orkain," suggested Chelk. "I must tell Vjann. She knows too much about us."

We disconnected, and I played with Rixo while Chelk reported to Vjann.

"Are you going out to find her?" I asked when he returned.

"No, we attack the cavern tomorrow."

"What if she's there?" I kept the volume low.

He shrugged. "She's decided. We need to attack while we can."

When Chelk returned from putting Rixo to bed, I worried. "He's still not recovered if he slept so quickly."

"It was still a fight. Don't stress," he replied.

"Is the shower running?" I worried again.

"I'm drawing a bath for you."

My brow furrowed. I couldn't hide my smile. No one had drawn a bath for me since I was a child.

"Wait here."

I waited on the couch while Chelk retrieved a palmful of fah. He eyed me and the amount in his hand, as if he meant to season me properly. Moments later my fah bath was ready. Chelk's brawny arms slid underneath me. I was in the air before I could stand. He was strong. I couldn't fight him.

A pile of toys lurked in the corner, but the bath and surrounding area were clear and welcoming. The dried fah leaves had expanded into delicate pink petals. Their jasmine scent danced with the steam and invigorated my senses. Placed upon the tiled edge of the tub, Chelk helped me undress and into my broth bath.

"What else can I get you?" he asked.

"You," I suggested in the oversized tub. "And a couple of glasses of fage?"

He hid a smile as he disappeared. I scrubbed well, so I could keep an air of mystery with my new lover.

I gave him no such privacy, watching him strip to his underpants when he returned. His skin was velvety smooth, emerald green, and taut over his thick muscles. The water was hotter for him. He tolerated it well, shoulders going slack.

I drew soaff bubbles over them, his back, and arms. He stared at my breasts. I pressed them into his hands for him to wash, goosebumps erupting on my flesh. The stars that spun inside his irises mirrored his horns, mesmerizing and strange. I bubbled with happiness.

He lowered his head and kissed me. His warmth poured over me like a warm shower. We figured out our lips and four tongues, and things got heated. His fingers spread my slick between my legs. He treasured each bit of skin with ardent kisses and nibbles and grazes of teeth.

The tub drained around us. Our mouths rarely separated; we didn't stay for the entire drying cycle. He laid me on the bed, where our height difference became more manageable.

His massive hands traveled across my damp skin, exploring every inch of me. He sucked sinfully on my breasts, sunk his tongues between them. He was so much larger and powerful. His kisses trailed between my breasts, across my stomach, and along the joints of my legs and hips.

Encouraged by my moans, he left marks on my skin and sucked my nipples into swollen peaks. Seeing such a large man at my breast was empowering. He differed from anyone I'd been with. While I had often seen Chelk shirtless, I had never seen him this close or been able to touch him wherever I wanted. His muscles had muscles. Corded and tough, they radiated from his center, drawing my fingers there, between his pecs, down his washboard abs.

Being his first human was liberating. He didn't know how skinny or smooth-skinned I should be. This was an experience unique to us, forever our own. It was slow, sensual, and powerful. I loved his breath on my skin. He massaged and kissed my legs. He nibbled up and down my thighs, staying close to my center, and his horns grazing my thighs felt feral and forbidden. My toes curled again, and he hadn't even licked into my center yet.

The first roll of his tongue across my knot of nerves was both a relief and another level of energy. My hips rocked against his face. A heavy hand held me. He breathed on my clit and kissed my entrance. I lost track as he plied me with his tongues. We blurred together. On my elbows, I admired him between my legs, gingerly lapping at my cunt. I caressed his rounded horns. He drank from my fountain.

He grunted and told me how sweet I tasted. "I want to make you come."

He stared up eagerly for instructions. "I want more of your tongue," I requested, despite feeling wonderful.

No one ever asked me what I wanted. As commanded, he pushed deep into me. My channel tightened around me. His tongue danced in my pussy and across my clit. Stuck for a moment, he wrenched his tongue free of my tight pussy before pressing back into me as I clenched further and came.

His tongue fought to stay in me. His nose dug into my clitoris. My cunt fucking vibrated. I'd never felt such intensity. He mumbled sweet, love-drunk words against my thighs, and when I opened my eyes, the universe spun around me. Toes I didn't remember curling relaxed. I pulled away, my skin sensitive as hell.

"I've got you," he said, before pulling me back to his mouth. His hands were on my hips and ass. His mouth was hot and pulsing.

Did Xavian women have multiple orgasms? Fortunately, he didn't seem to expect anything from me. He savored his meal. The tension in my muscles melted like butter. His touch became tolerable, then enjoyable. I doubt I could come again. I never needed to again.

Three tongues wrapped into a single member, painting my clit and cunt. Arching my back extended the sensation. I rubbed against his slick, thick tongue, imagining his hard cocks parallel to my entrance. I wondered whether he'd fit inside me. More of my wetness joined Chelk's saliva. My eyes soaked him in, his head bobbing and giving me every good thing, but there was no way—

I was falling to pieces in his mouth. He controlled my whole lower body, working his face into my pussy. On fire, I encouraged him to keep going. Warned him not to stop. I controlled the wheel, grabbing his horns, and pulling him deeper between my legs.

Chapter Twenty-Four
Must Go

Chelk

I soaked in every curve and joint of her body. How soft her skin was. How Xavian soaff smelled on her. Between her legs, her heady scent tempted me to devour her. I curled my tongues along her folds and teased juices from her. Sweet, complex, and layered—she was a feast for a chef. Each gentle moan made my cocks leap, pressed against the mattress.

Her legs caged me. They tightened around me as I twirled my tongues on her clit and meandered through sensitive valleys. Her cunt was the most delicious thing I ever tasted. I couldn't get enough. I traveled low and licked her asshole.

"Oh!" she said, surprised.

I withdrew my tongues. "Something you disliked?" I asked.

"Well, um, no," she said. "The guys I date don't go there, but you aren't the guys I usually date."

"Did you enjoy it?"

She nodded, biting her lip, dropping her head in resignation. I returned my tongues gently. Sex was full of surprises. I'd take care to prepare her.

"Jesus," she said. Her thighs muffled the call.

Was she remembering another human at her cunt? I withdrew and spoke away from her swollen labia.

"Who is he? I'm Chelk."

"What? Oh, no. It's a swear. It's not someone's name. Well, no one you need to worry about." She laughed and touched my face to reassure me. "You're amazing."

"Jesus is a good word?"

"Yes. Now, please…"

Layla pushed me to her waiting pussy, hot and needy. She wanted me to continue, then she shouldn't have called someone else's name. I would teach her.

"Will this make you cum?" I asked, giving her a long, quick lick along her seam.

"Maybe," she whispered.

"Or, do you want me inside?" I asked, inserting a tongue into her channel.

"Jesus!" she exclaimed.

One of my tongues traveled to her clit and lapped against it, my other braced inside her. When I licked from both sides, a whimper escaped her closed mouth.

I prepared her small, tight holes for my cocks. They dilated and softened with work. I stretched her with my tongues. I loved her taste, her silky feel. Everything was wet. I sipped from her, memorizing her flavors, and wondering if I'd ever tasted anything so exciting prior. I was certain I hadn't. Nothing like it existed on Xavia.

I explored with my sensitive and skilled tongues. I listened to her building need. Her muscles and channel tightened, tensed, and relaxed. With every shift in pressure, she responded—an intense connection I relished.

I enjoyed the evening, worshiping every part of her body. I could fall asleep on these thighs with my tongue nestled in her warmth and my nose in her curls, much coarser than the curls on her head, although they were of the same color. Besides the hair on her head, she had eyebrows, her pubic tuft which embarrassed her, and much finer hair on her body. Just as her long hair could cover her breasts or hide her cute eyes, the dark hair hid the juicy flesh I plunged my face into now.

"Your tongues are so long," she cooed.

I tickled her deep to show how long. The vibration spread through her, manifesting in a wiggle of her upper body. With greedy hands, I grabbed ass, thigh, and tummy and held her to my jaw.

"Oh, f—, keep that up. That feels nice…" she trailed off as I kept the rhythm and motion.

I lapped at her flesh and drew cries from her lips.

"Hah-zah!" my son shouted from the other room, startling me. The terror and desperation in his cry haunted zaratas. How long had he been crying?

"Hah-zah!"

I untangled myself from her legs, apologizing and calling out in different languages.

In his room, he sat upright, with big eyes and a gaping maw. I picked him up and hugged him to my chest.

"It's okay. I'm here. Hah-zah's here."

He wasn't burning up. Maybe a nightmare. I tended him alone until he fell asleep. Successfully laying him back down, I left for Layla's bed. I wanted her to be beside her, even if she slept.

* * *

The next morning, my blossoming family remained perfect and fragile. I had to leave to attack the cavern. My family needed protection. Vjann built our military from nothing, and had my respect and loyalty. Lian needed supervision, and someone needed to keep Kane grounded.

Rixo dumped over a cup of thick white liquid.

"What is that?" I said, mortified, looking for something to dry it.

"Oh, I'm sorry!" she said.

She was experimenting again. I mopped up the mess and took it to the kitchen. I returned with a small box of pigmented chalk. Zade used them to mark the mines. I explained that she might be able to dilute them to create watercolors.

Layla's eyes welled with tears. I wasn't expecting that. She muttered her thanks. I felt huge, confident, and floaty. That part I expected.

The air was heavy, except where Layla touched me. It's as if the rain showers, the clouds never touched her. No matter what was happening, her entire being glowed. She brought happiness, as her paintings did. I didn't want such a magnificent being's happiness to dim.

"Paint me something," I said.

"What should I paint?"

I thought about how small her life was here.

"Paint Earth."

"Earth's enormous."

"Okay, only the parts you liked."

She laughed, enjoying the challenge. "I will paint something I liked about Earth."

A pang of regret reminded me she might go back. As wonderful as the day was, it passed in a whirlwind of cooking and chasing Rixo. I told the story of a young Xavian who climbed our tallest mountain. Layla told him a story about a wolf hunting three pigs. He fell asleep, but I heard the third pig survived in a brick house.

"Maybe it should be an underground house, not a brick house. And…what's a wolf?" I asked once we'd left Rixo's room.

"It's a dog's wild ancestor. A predator."

"This is a bedtime story on Earth?" I asked. "Earth doesn't seem very nice."

"The people on it…they're not all bad," she defended.

"Are any else like you?"

I didn't want Rixo to suffer like Layla had on Earth. She told me about racial and gender discrimination. How much more differently would they treat Rixo because he wasn't their same species? Our home was here. Layla's, too.

"What do you mean?"

Her smile reinforced my point, even as I searched for the words.

"So optimistic. I keep telling myself it's because you're naive and haven't experienced tragedy, but you have."

"Everyone's experienced tragedy…or will. It's how we heal and survive that matters."

Her smile hid secrets I coveted.

There was no one like her. Stella and I hadn't meshed well. We irritated each other. Layla was gentle, loving, and compassionate. I enjoyed basking in her glow. I enjoyed worshiping her pussy too. Everything about her was perfect.

I didn't want Earth or Layla on it. I kissed her and remained silent. Our relationship was so new. Telling someone you want to spend eternity with them before going off to war wasn't kind. I wouldn't wish rotha on anyone.

Chapter Twenty-Five
Fear

Layla

The next morning seemed to go faster than any of them had. Chelk gave Rixo a hug that had the little boy fussing to be put down. Surprising both me and Rixo, Chelk pulled me into his arms, a distinct show of affection in front of his son. He kissed me, and Rixo giggled, jumping into the fray. Kiss interrupted, but cute. Chelk kissed the top of Rixo's head and said his goodbyes, having delayed as long as he could.

"What do you want to do today?" I asked Rixo.

"Swim!"

I laughed. "Maybe we can fill up the big tub today. Do you want to do that now?"

"Paint!"

That was definitely my favorite of the choices today. We could experiment with binders for Zade's chalk. For Rixo, we didn't need a strong binder. We needed things to stay washable. Chelk had given me an assignment to paint—something I loved about Earth was easy. It was silly and basic, but I loved painting flowers. If there were a god or goddess, they'd have created a lot of different flowers…not just one flower but millions, and different colors, varieties, and all pretty in their own time, then fading. Flowers were temporary, but they also came back every year.

I would paint him daisies, my favorite flower, and they'd remind him of my endless sunshine and optimism, or whatever he called it. I pictured the composition in my head, and the colors needed—yellows, greens, and blue. It would be a field and a sunset…an open field isn't something we could enjoy with the Orkain here. It signified something dangerous, like prey out in the wild. I'd put a picnic blanket and have all three of us lying there out in the open, enjoying the Earth's sunshine. That felt more like an alien world than anything else.

First, we would play with the colors and the spread and all of that. Rixo enjoyed using his fingers. I withheld items like tree sap that had potential but too messy for Rixo. He enjoyed using them like markers to draw on the paper.

The settit rang. Cassie was on the other end. I was just thinking that Zade hadn't been called in for the action today.

"It seems like something big, huh?" said Cassie. Her Zade had been called away too. It seemed like they were going for the cave again. "How are you feeling?"

We were using toddler-safe talk. Cash was too young, but Rixo fed off of us, and we didn't want to test his understanding. I took stock of my body.

"I'm nervous but nothing else." None of those rotha pains that I'd heard expressed. "When did rotha kick in for you?" I wondered if it would ever happen to me, and what it meant if it didn't.

"Hm, I didn't know it was rotha…and I had so many other conflicting feelings. Cash."

I remembered nodding. I had my own complications.

"Way before then, but I wasn't ready to experience them," she admitted.

"I'm just wondering what it's supposed to feel like."

"You like him, right?" she asked.

I did, but I liked all the men I'd been in relationships with. That didn't mean it lasted. "I do…"

"But, it doesn't have to be rotha if you like him."

I tried to wrap my head around that. Now that I knew rotha existed…that my body could grow love tattoos for someone…why would I ever settle for something beneath that?

"He is okay with it. He's done it before," she said, talking about Kaytor.

I nodded as if to speed up this part of the conversation. It made me uncomfortable.

"But now does he just want someone to help him?" I asked.

"Do you get that vibe from him?"

"No… but doesn't rotha improve fertility?"

"We don't know jack squat about rotha and fertility. It's all an experiment."

She was right. Sara had announced her pregnancy, but she was still carrying her child. We all hoped for a healthy birth, curious how our species would blend. What if rotha was just our bodies going haywire, and we weren't optimal mates at all with any Xavians?

Cassie and I kept are settits connected even when we got up to do different things. It felt good to have someone "there" even if they weren't. Settits had a sort of call-waiting so we wouldn't miss any alerts. Like a little lifeline, especially when there were so few of us. We were kept isolated by the Orkain, constantly on lockdown. And we were so far from Earth. Cassie was right. I wanted them. I didn't need them like they needed me, but I loved and wanted them all the same.

Rixo didn't eat much for lunch, and he gave up all appearances of eating dinner, mostly crying for his father. I wasn't able to stop him from running around the house either. He also wouldn't take 'wait until you digest anything you ate' before wanting me to turn him upside down and tickle him. Thankfully, nothing came back up, although he did take some quiet time after that. I played Earth music. We probably should have brought some children's programming, but I doubt anyone expected to be entertaining children on this trip. He liked watching all the humans in *Telefunctional*, but it's not really a show for kids. Eventually he'd understand the words, and I'd have to come up with reasons the adult jokes were funny without actually explaining them.

I wondered what Rixo would be like when he got older, and if he'd like to be a big brother. He would probably like the company, seeing as we didn't get out to meet kids his age very often. How much crazier would this house be? Would they ever sleep at the same time? After a bit, Little Rixo fell asleep without prompting, still recovering from his illness, and I pulled out my paint supplies.

Chelk had gathered the chalk from Zade under my nose and ensured there was always a fresh stack of paper…difficult when his child liked to mark up all available pages. Something about a fresh stack was caring and provided endless possibilities. Lots of flowers. When I pulled out a fresh sheet, it was soft and smooth, and suddenly I wasn't sketching flowers but that waterfall and pool. I recalled the first time I saw it. I hadn't known it existed, and to me, we stumbled upon an oasis, a place to dip, dive and be safe from the Orkain. It was a surprise sanctuary.

That's how I felt about this home. As crazy as it was. As insane as it was to have Orkain flying overhead. Here, especially when Chelk was here, the home was full and safe. I submerged my hopes and dreams into the painting's flowing water, ripples, and rush. I could bathe in its safety, and Chelk had led me there.

I watched Rixo snooze, and I couldn't wait for Chelk to come home so we could start the rest of our lives together. Nothing bad could happen to him out there…that's not what a fairy tale was supposed to be about. And if he was my true love, he couldn't just not come back. Halfway through the painting, I stepped back. It wasn't perfect, but it was all the things that I liked and none of the things that I didn't.

And I imagined Chelk and me making out in the water. Him holding me close, and everything else being washed away. I painted us there. Small, not detailed. You couldn't tell what we were doing, just being close, just enjoying and resting in our sanctuary. I was thankful that Chelk was trying to make that dream come true. And I still remained scared to death that he might never come back.

Chapter Twenty-Six
Attack

Chelk

Vjann and Zade had surveyed the rest of the cavern and verified Bonnie's information, even if she herself had escaped. No one had seen her. With the cave's location compromised and the rain slowing, they'd move to a more secure location soon.

Kane hadn't arrived; I wasn't last, for once. Unable to delay, Vjann led the completed groups to the cliff. Zade's presence meant we still planned to use explosives. If Kane didn't arrive soon, we'd be part of the clean-up instead of the fight. I dug the toe of my boot into the leaf litter while Lian sat adjusting the straps on his.

Kane arrived with brows and horns stitched close and no apology. I fell in behind him. Lian behind me, tapping the shield on my back. We caught up with the group that arrived at our original meeting spot. I expected the others to be covering the top and other vantage points. I wished for placement at the top of the cliff-face. From there, we could drop and land on an Orkain as it flew out. No bases needed. I could fly. Lian could fly. Kane could too.

Before I could discuss it, Orkain and the pair of Xavians bolted from the cave. They raced as the lower part of the cliff exploded. I shielded Lian and myself. My ears rang as I followed Kane's charge to the ripped-open Orkain roost. More Orkain than our teams could handle spilled from the hole.

I set up my shield according to his directions.

"Yi, yi, yi!" Kane counted the rhythm. I caught Lian's foot and boosted his launch. His arms flung madly, catching a wing. They tumbled to the ground where the three of us attacked. The Orkain seized and trembled as it died.

Fryyre. I swallowed bile and turned toward Kane's yell for the next. Bloodied and dirtied, Lian and I set up for the next. He landed, digging his heels squarely into the squawking, surprised Orkain. He stabbed into the base of its skull, pulling the blade from the creature as they dropped from the sky.

Vjann motioned us forward, completing our first round of attack. We moved over the cave's destroyed entrance. Orkain and Xavian lie dead on the ground. Among the rubble were the remains of someone from the cliff top.

From the darkness, an Orkain launched into Vjann. He hugged the creature and fell backward with its momentum. It flew, dragging Vjann. I didn't pity it. Vjann was a heavy man.

"Bases!" he shouted.

Lian and Duncan flew, but only Duncan landed. Another beast struck Lian. He swung his body and kicked at its chin, trying to get free. Kane and I raced to recover him. Kane grabbed Lian, and the Orkain could not sustain its low flight. I climbed toward its head, wrenched on its horn. It bucked underneath me, screeching, changing direction to throw me. Even as my blade sank into its neck, it flopped. I fought to stay on—a mistake. We half fell and half slid into the deep bottom of the cavern.

When I came to, the dead Orkain lay on my legs, which had gone numb. Lian and Kane were missing. I hoped they fell on more favorable ground.

"Haellea stupid-head!" shouted Kane above me.

"I was saving you, stupid-head," I said, although I'm not sure my voice traveled as far.

"I'll take Lian to Heljin, then we'll return for you. That alright?"

Lian was the owner of the sobs. At least it meant his lungs were okay. "It'll be all right. I'm fine," I lied. Fine enough.

He ripped a handful of glow-plants from the tunnels and tossed them to me. I wish he hadn't. Besides the most recent Orkain, I lay on the bones of my people. Clean, picked bones pricked my conscience and planted forever in my dreams. Meanwhile, I readied to roll the heavy mass off my legs. There'd been too many for us. We'd been too slow and too sloppy. Escaped Orkain could return at any point. I needed to free myself. Rixo and Layla needed me to teach them how to read. And I needed Rixo and Layla to keep me from the depths.

I might've blacked out while moving the Orkain, but he was off my mangled right leg. Even with two healthy legs, it'd be impossible to climb. The nauseating pain and shock at least kept me from reflecting on the people lost around me, and one responsible slumped amongst them.

Where were Kaytor's bones? If we'd been rotha mates, could I seek them? Grief and pain mingled and shuffled time. In another moment, Kane was there, cursing my weight and dragging me onto a sled.

"Don't forget my shield," I mumbled to the stupidhead before I passed out again.

Chapter Twenty-Seven
Injury

Layla

I tossed and turned on the beds and urish, aching for him. I'd scrubbed everything shiny. At least Chelk would return to a clean home.

Hopefully soon.

I pulled my paint from their tall cubby and mulled over the colors. Detailing the helena berries on either side of the trail, I practiced lines I'd tell Rixo in the morning.

Hah-zah went to work early. He says hi, and he loves you.

Hah-zah is still at work. I'm not sure when he'll be home, but what do you want to do while we wait?

My heart ached. I scratched at the dried paint on my forearms where I'd leaned. This wasn't paint. Running water in the sink, I questioned the soft knock on the door. My heart dropped. Chelk wouldn't knock.

I escorted the tall, soaking Xavian from the rain. "Kane?" I asked.

He confirmed. "Chelk hurt his leg. He's at Heljin's."

I motioned to the urish, but he declined. He turned to leave, rain still dripping from his beard.

"No, tell me how hurt. Take me to him."

If Xavians could roll their eyes, he would have. He gestured at the dark rain he'd come from and said 'no' in both languages.

"I'll go without you." I warned him, handing him a glass of water and a handful of dried fruit.

"You should stay here. Stay with the little one."

No, I needed to go to Chelk. It hadn't just been nervousness. I pulled on my sleeve and showed Kane the lightning marks that now tattooed my inner arm. "Please take me to him."

The marks changed Kane's mind.

"You are rotha mates. Good. He'll need you. Pack quickly."

I changed and packed a change of clothes for everyone and a couple of soft toys. I laced my boots and put on a too-big jacket. Kane carried the bag and Rixo. Every step in the dark, rainy jungle was tough, but the pain I recognized as rotha now drove me forward. I didn't need Kane to navigate, though I was thankful for him. He kept Rixo dry and warm and me safe as we journeyed to Chelk. If he couldn't come home, we'd go to him.

Heljin had finished Chelk's surgery when we arrived. Kane kept Rixo occupied while Heljin explained how extensive the trauma to Chelk's leg had been. He amputated it, but Chelk could keep his knee and part of his lower leg. Recovery would be faster and his prosthesis less complicated. Heljin recommended an engineer named Arekh.

Once I tended Rixo, I brought him into the room with us and sang them both a Xavian lullaby Chelk had taught me. Xavian lullabies were full of love and hope, not cribs falling or sending children to bed without food. Chelk lay motionless. His face was vacant and slack. The bedsheet fell where his calf and foot were not. Snuggled next to him, my heart sang more than a lullaby, finding home in his scent of cinnamon and exhaustion. The uncertainty of the future terrified me, but I was presently at home.

Chapter Twenty-Eight
Loss

Chelk

The familiar darkness dissolved into an unfamiliar ceiling. I was neither at home nor in the cavern. I drifted even within my body. The pain in my leg felt distant. Layla was at my side, a small, warm, unexpected salve. We must be in the hospital.

My slightest movement woke her, a testament to how long I'd been still. Something inside me stirred as she did.

"You're waking up from surgery. Everything is okay. You're going to be all right."

"Surgery?"

"How much do you remember?" The skin between her eyes crinkled.

Not enough, apparently.

"When did you get here?" I asked. Rixo slept in a pile of blankets on the floor. I didn't remember them arriving.

"Kane escorted us after he got you to surgery."

"He shouldn't have done that. You should have stayed home." My son too.

"In surgery…part of your foot was already gone…Heljin saved what he could."

I craned my neck where the blanket fell short on my right side. No foot, ankle, most of my calf. Useless as a base for Lian. I'd never serve again.

"I'm sorry."

She was? That made two of us.

"I missed you so much. I l—love you."

"Don't say that." She was in love with the old me, the whole me. We didn't know who I'd be now. "You don't know how this will change me."

"Because you've lost your leg? You're still the strongest person I know."

Wow, she was carelessly optimistic. She'd speak differently if she remembered her other options. "You'll be happier with Moto or safer on Earth."

She possessed every possibility this world held, plus Earth's. Why should she become mine and my son's caregiver?

"Babe, let me show you something," Layla pulled her arms from around my chest and out from under the blanket. Rotha's marks crossed her forearms like reverse lightning.

"On my calves too. Our calves…" she breathed.

I threw the blanket off us. My forearms and left leg had matching patterns, thick and solid. Had my discarded limb had marks before being cut from my body? My anger burned against the limb and body that had betrayed me.

The pain in my leg was nothing compared to the guilt in my heart. I pulled the covers back. Heljin had been correct. Those marks were new, extending from underneath the bandages up my leg. Marks on my left leg reflected what couldn't be seen on my right.

My body had chosen surgery to blossom into rotha marks. Lying on my bed with one and a half legs and still enough pain seeping through my consciousness to color every single one of my thoughts, the arcing lines reminded me of chains. It's as if my pitiful body knew we'd need another to survive. Rotha's marks secured her to someone who'd always need help. I felt betrayed by my body and my heart. Layla was my everything, yet this union would prove her ruin. I needed so much of her help. I needed her. And I worried she'd resent me for it.

"Don't feel obligated to stay with me."

"What? Are you serious? I wish to be with you. I want to help you."

Help? "I'm not a pity case. I don't need your help."

"I'm sorry. Maybe I said it wrong. I'm here for whatever happens."

She put closed lips on mine. She wanted me to let her in, and I couldn't do it. Pain shot through me as I moved to sit upright.

"Stop, you're not supposed to do that," said Layla. "What do you need? I'll get it."

She jumped up on her two good feet—nearly hopping. I saw green through my tears.

"I need to pee," I said, biting back my anger.

Layla handed me a container and left to give me privacy. I wouldn't be able to tend to my son when he woke. I couldn't even pee without help.

* * *

The next morning Kane arrived and helped me onto a sled.

"Like last time," he said.

155

I don't remember.

Rixo hopped onto my chest, pressing all the air out of it. He laughed as I swallowed my pain. I didn't want Kane's help, but I needed it. I wanted to go home and sulk.

Skies cleared, but we took a long route home for the sled…for me. Layla followed behind the sled while Kane pulled. Rixo bounded among us, "helping." I tried to keep my conversation with Kane as muted as possible.

"We destroyed the cave. They won't be able to use it anymore."

"How many got away, though?"

"Too many. They waited too long after rescuing Bonnie."

"Bonnie said they'd turn on each other."

"We found bodies of Orkain we didn't kill. But I wouldn't trust what she said because she ran away."

I cursed, and Rixo came bounding to me. Bonnie must not have thought we were rescuing her from the Orkain. In her eyes, we were abducting her. I was only following orders, but I wouldn't anymore. The rest of my life and regrets loomed.

Once placed into my bed and Kane's farewell, I worried I'd be in the bed forever. I tried to get up multiple times, but Layla was on watch. She overtook me before I could even finish shuffling to the edge of the bed. She watched me as a parent would. In her hand she held a children's book for Rixo as if she would now put me to bed with it. Eventually she had to leave me alone to bathe Rixo and put him to bed.

Meanwhile, I wanted to unwrap and check my stump. I eyed the room for the hand mirror, unreachable from the bed. I was as silent as I could be, but Layla's ears were as skilled as they were beautifully curved.

"Don't get up!" Her voice strained from the other room.

"I'm never going to be someone who doesn't try," I shot.

Her head popped into the room. I envied her mobility. She bit her lip. Her eyes bored into mine. We were both so hard-headed.

"I know. I love that about you. Please give yourself a rest for one night. Then, if you need to physically push yourself, let me stand by. Now what do you need right now?"

Besides a functioning leg? "The mirror."

"Oh, I can check your leg in a moment. Do you need a mirror?"

Why did it matter that she could see my wound? I was the one who needed to take care of it. I'd need to learn for when she was gone.

She walked with ease through the room. My back teeth ground. She set the mirror reflection side down beside the bed and began pulling on my covers.

I yanked them back. "Leave."

She stared me down again. This time I wasn't budging. I wanted to see this for myself, alone.

"Why won't you let me help you?"

The question stung. I didn't know the answer. I didn't want to deal with her or any of it right now.

"Leave," I commanded.

"Chelk…" she fell silent for a moment, undecided. "I'm going to give you some privacy and space, but I'll be out in the living room. I'm not *leaving*."

She picked up a children's book about a saf lost in the jungle looking for its mother before stepping out of the room and closing the door behind her. It's what I wanted—to be alone and miserable.

I didn't need to unwrap it. Undoing the covers to expose the bandaged stump was enough. I tossed the mirror. It landed where my leg used to be, reflecting the whole in place of the lost. My heart thudded heavy in my chest.

Chapter Twenty-Nine
Space

Layla

He wanted space and privacy. I needed him to not get up, to give it one day's rest. One day!

He wasn't a child. I examined Rixo's book still in my death grip. The title translated to *The Tiny Saf.* Sadly, no one had illustrated the book. I'd never seen one.

Recalling Sara had mentioned their saf, I called her settit.

I regretted it when she asked about Chelk.

"He's home? That's a lot on you, caring for him and Rixo. I know that's not what you agreed to."

Chelk had said the same. I didn't want it to be true.

"Apparently rotha disagrees." I pulled back my sleeve.

Sara breathed a curse. "That's a lot going on, girl."

"You're telling me."

Sara's peach lip caught between her teeth for a moment. "I guess that's why they sent Chelk home."

"Where else would he go?" I asked, curious.

"Gulshan has space for you all. Everyone there can help out. You don't have to do it alone. Y'all can think about it."

I thanked her and then giggled, remembering why I had called. I picked up the book to show her.

"Are you reading that to Rixo?"

"Once I get good at it."

We both shared a laugh.

"I've been doing the same! I'm trying to be smart enough when this kid gets here," she patted her rounding belly.

"You've got more time than me. Mine already recognizes as many letters as I do."

She smiled at "mine" and so did I. He wasn't mine. He looked nothing like me, but he was mine. I loved him.

"You and Vance have a saf, right?"

"Oh, yes, Moyuki."

She grabbed the settit and tilted it at the floor. By her feet was a small black panther with long fur. At the sound of her name, she looked up drowsily. Oh, I wanted one!

"She was shy at first, but now she follows me everywhere. I hope she doesn't eat my baby."

She was joking, I hoped. Cats were hunters on Earth, and this one was large. Hopefully, it had a dog's personality—loyal and affectionate. "Where did he get it?"

"It was his neighbor's, but she died, so he began taking care of it. I don't know if they breed them or just…capture them from the wild when they're young? I never asked. I don't want another," she laughed. "She is an excellent foot warmer and protector, though."

I didn't know if I wanted one that big. She was as big as my toddler. I had imagined something much smaller…I guess that's why the book was called *The Tiny Saf* and not *The Averaged Sized Saf.*

Even though I didn't have pets on Earth, family farms and animals still surrounded me in the Midwest. I missed them and I began imagining my saf-filled future here with Chelk and Rixo.

If only Chelk would have me.

Rotha didn't awaken my desire to be a part of his family, a part of his priorities, and a part of his life. I already loved Chelk, how he carried himself, and kept his family safe. He'd lost so much and grieved. In these moments, I could wait patiently. I looked toward the future with him, with Rixo, and a family all my own. We were in hard times, but we would find a way together through them.

As much as I wanted to help him, he had to accept that help. I was being disrespectful by dictating how he should recover. Even if I felt we could manage on our own, I'd offer him the opportunity to go to Gulshan's…even alone.

Chapter Thirty
Nights Together

Chelk

Layla drew a warm sponge along the rotha marks on my arm.

"Do you try to wash them off?" I asked her.

"No, I love them. I *want* my rotha marks because before them, I wouldn't believe you belonged to me."

She wanted us, me. She shouldn't. Not with my limb loss and the Orkain's reign. I'd failed her as much as I'd failed Rixo's mother.

She took a deep breath. "And I wouldn't feel confident enough to tell you about Gulshan's offer to have any of us stay."

Rixo and I could stay with Gulshan. Layla could stay with Moto or return to Earth in a few months. We both had options. She offered this to me, despite the rotha marks, despite the injury, despite her feelings. I appreciated that.

"Do you want to be with me?"

My voice cracked. "Of course, you're my mate. Our *zaratas* are forever bound." I struggled to find the word in English.

"What is zarata?"

"Inside us. Every living thing has a zarata. It is what makes us individual and unique."

"Is it a part of the body?" she asked.

"It is inside our core."

"I don't know if we have an exact translation. Maybe soul. It's like the intangible part of people. Or we say we love people with our hearts. That's the organ that pumps blood."

"You're all of that and more, but it's not fair to you."

"It's not fair to keep me from my rotha mate."

That was true. "I can't keep anything from you. I will give you anything you want. Unless it's a right foot because I don't have that."

A laugh escaped Layla's lips before her hand clamped over it. We waited for the baby's cry. Her still eyes glistened with laughter, brightening my dark, tired zarata. We were lucky.

"Do we want to live with Gulshan temporarily?" It was unfair to ask her to care for me and my child alone.

"No, I want to adjust to our home. I prefer to be home."

I wanted the same. Her fingers slipped through my hair, dividing sections for braiding. We spoke late into the night, filled with silly jokes, and she confessed she was drawing in one of Rixo's books.

"I love you with all of me."

"Both feet?" I joked. "I love you with both feet too…somewhere."

"Stop it with the feet."

Then her lips brushed the side of my neck, kissing away stray hairs. I kissed her forehead. She and her zarata, heart, blood, whatever were mine now.

Heljin told me it helped to have goals in recovery. I wanted to cook dinner for my family. Every day became an opportunity to test my balance and strength. I hated sitting still. By the afternoon my leg had swollen and impeded cooking dinner.

I had a pile of pichini to prepare. Removing them from their pods was easy, unless you balanced on one leg. Little things took so much effort.

Layla's soft footsteps landed behind me. Fryyre, she'd put an end to this. Didn't she understand how important this was to me?

"It's not hurting," I lied.

"Why don't we do it together then?"

Not my goal, but progress. She brought two chairs into the kitchen. I dropped into the seat, declining her help with my leg. I could do it myself. It hurt like hell either way.

Fryyre.

"What are we cooking? How can I help?"

I pointed to the pichini. She tossed me one, and I showed her how to pull apart the pods. Layla's first try shot a pichini so hard at the ceiling that Rixo came to investigate the *pop* and laughter. Rixo climbed onto my lap after finding the lost pichini underneath one of my chairs. Layla so gracefully put him on her hip that neither Rixo nor I thought to argue. She handed me the bowl of pichini before turning on the stove.

I feared *this?*

No, I feared loss, but who am I to argue with fate? My losses had brought me here with the knowledge and ability to love someone deeply. She was my life, even if it made little sense or wasn't fair. She was mine. Rotha's marks meant *forever, but* I didn't need them to realize Layla was my best chance at a wonderful and happy life. I would care for her and Rixo, and that meant healing my stump and my mental health. I'd been the best soldier I could be. Now I had to be the best Xavian, father, and mate. Kaytor taught me how to love. She'd taught me how to love Layla. I was capable.

She added oil to the hot pan, just as I had taught her. It wasn't standing over crackling oil and feeling my beard singe, but I was proud. This worked. She reached for the pichini and I pulled her in for a kiss. Rixo slid down her leg with a giggle, running into the next room.

"Come back, sous chef!" she called.

"Shoe theft!" shouted Rixo, running back through the kitchen.

"Please slow down," said Layla, unable to physically catch him. He was fast.

He came around the next lap with Layla's shoe in hand. I grabbed it from him, surprised at how worn it was. They were not enduring the jungle.

"These need to be replaced."

"Oh, yeah, probably. The problem is that my feet are so narrow compared to Xavian feet."

I hadn't realized Layla lacked necessities. "I'm so sorry. What else do you need?" Where else was my care lacking? I was too focused on her safety.

"The clothes are wonderful. Gulshan tailors them, which is so sweet. I'm running out of paint, but that's not really a priority..."

It was to me. Anything to make her happy.

"How about those pichini, then?" she asked.

I'd forgotten. I handed the bowl to her. With a flick of her wrist, she tossed them into the hot pan, where they rapidly jumped out with loud pops. Layla jumped back with a shout of her own.

"The pan's for the fish!" I said, dodging pichini. Rixo promptly joined the commotion, shouting because he wasn't yet the center. Layla grabbed him, changing his direction abruptly, scooping him up from the potential burn hazard.

Left to fend for myself, it was less my leg and more my uproarious laughter that had me struggling from the chairs. I righted myself and, ducking, turned the heat off the stove and moved the pan. It cooled, and my family, who had abandoned me, were soon back in the kitchen, picking surprisingly sticky pichini from the ground and walls. We tossed them around with much laughter and glee. Eventually, I had to sit and hold the bowl as the others clambered for the popped food.

Layla spooned the remaining pichini from the oil and prepared a salad instead. I didn't approve of every vegetable, but she "dressed" them with a sauce of salt, pepper, oil, and vinegar. Infusing the oils could give endless flavor possibilities. If I had the pub house …

It was a stupid dream. Dining out was an unnecessary danger, though people still needed to eat. Did Drex or Vance need a cook? I didn't blame them, but I'd grow bitter interacting with them daily. The reason my life and family looked so different was the Orkain's fault, not theirs. There was no point in wishing the Orkain gone. This was our new life.

I tried to catch one of Rixo's wild pichini throws and half the pichini sloshed from the bowl. Rixo appreciated returning them to the bowl in handfuls, yelling "goal" and "slam dunk," which were words Layla had taught us. I doubted Rixo nor I understood the precise meaning, but Rixo said them with such enthusiasm, it mattered little.

Slam dunk.

Chapter Thirty-One
New Love

Layla

Chelk's laughter over my explosive mistake lifted my heart and soul. Instead of kicking me out of the kitchen, he even let me experiment with my salad equivalent. My rotha marks caught my eye. I bit the giddiness from my lips. Things finally felt like they were turning.

Watching Chelk and Rixo find joy in cooking, not just dinner, showed me how important cooking was for Chelk, his recovery, his life. He loved this. My mind reeled with opportunities to bring him more of this joy.

"I don't know if you remember, but when you were first hurt, people gave us food. I want to send back cooked meals to thank them. Do you think we could do that?"

"I didn't realize that happened. Are these human traditions?"

"I guess so. Come to think of it, they were from human-Xavian couples."

Chelk spouted meal ideas, inspired by a new cooking opportunity. "I miss cooking large meals."

"You still could."

"What? If we make a big family?"

"Well, yeah, that, I guess." I choked.

So much of Chelk was coming alive. We couldn't speak freely with Rixo at our feet. I hid my joyous expression beneath my curls.

I ventured with another idea. "I was thinking you could cook for those who can't. You can cook a big dish as you did at the public house. We'll divide them and have them delivered to people's homes."

"This is something humans do?"

Xavians had learned to question human intentions and traditions.

"Not exactly, but these are special circumstances." Chelk needed purpose. "I bet people miss your meals."

A smile crept onto his face. "I will need your help."

"It's work we can do here. We'll be together."

"I want to deliver the meals."

This man. "We will get you a bike. You can be Meals-on-Wheels."

"What's a bike?" he asked before pulling me into a kiss, my curly hair falling into our faces, getting into both of our mouths.

That was fine. The affection was enough. We chatted about cooking and menus. He formed the first week's menu based on seasonal foods. We needed a diner list and their allergies

After a delicious salvaged dinner and a peaceful bedtime from Rixo, Chelk showed his typical irritated, grumpy side. He sat on the urish, digging his fingers into his thigh. "I swear my foot itches. It's been itching all day, and it's driving me crazy."

"Phantom pains," I said, sitting down beside him. I remembered the phenomenon.

"Phantom?"

"A phantom is like a ghost…a spirit or departed soul." I wasn't explaining it well. "Anyway, your brain still thinks your foot is there and assigns sensation to it."

"How do I fix it?"

I shrugged. "Maybe scratch it?" I slipped onto the floor in front of him. "Picture your foot and tell me where you want me to scratch it."

"That's silly…" he said, shaking his head.

"Sure, but try anyway. What's it going to hurt? Are you afraid I'm going to tickle you?" I launched into tickling the inner arch of his invisible foot.

He jumped from my attack and then fell into laughter. I fell over laughing, too. It took us a moment to regain our composure.

"Okay, let me figure out where it itches…" Chelk's voice lilted. He closed his eyes. "I'm imagining my weight of it on the ground. The itch isn't there. It's higher on the top of my foot or on my ankle."

"So, here?" I asked.

He opened his eyes and watched my movements with intent.

"Higher." After a moment, "Right there, yeah."

His face broke into a grin. I wasn't sure if he was just teasing me, but he at least appreciated the attention I was giving him and his itchy foot. I scratched the top of his foot and massaged near his stump, trying to appease his nerves.

"This is dumb, but will you use the hand mirror to reflect my foot?"

I jumped up to the mirror. That was a fantastic idea. I scratched his foot and his reflected foot for him.

"Thank you. That feels better somehow."

"You're very welcome," I said.

Released, I didn't want to stop touching him. I kissed his legs. He put an appreciative hand in my hair, trying to sweep the curls from my face. I assisted him, pulling it over my shoulder. Then, I assisted him with his shorts, pulling and twisting them off him. His cocks snaked over his waistband. They entwined as a single entity, then separated and gyrated. They stretched.

"That's crazy, all right," I said, hesitating.

Chelk leaned over to find his pants. I pushed him back.

"No, no, I'm sorry if I insulted you. I'm new to this."

The power dynamic shifted. His immobility empowered me to shower him with sexual attention, rather than clinical care. For both, I was new. I ran my hands along his thighs, much gentler than his abuse of them earlier. His cocks enlarged. I picked the largest, cupping the head and pulling lubricant down its velvety length. The lubricant was translucent and—flavorless. I licked and massaged him with my tongue.

My hands teased his other cocks, stroking them as I swirled my tongue around his tip and filled my mouth with him. When I tried to swallow, he groaned around his smirk. I gagged. Porn made it look easy. I slowed my sloppy enthusiasm to check for his approval.

"You're do—ing fine." He stumbled over his words.

He bulged and stretched my lips. I hollowed my cheeks and swallowed. His legs contracted. My black curls bobbed over his lap. I should have tied it up. His whole body swayed with my movements.

I squeezed his lurching cocks. They contorted as he climaxed. I tensed, though he didn't release any fluid.

He massaged my scalp with a hand caught in my tangles.

"Was that good?" I asked, easing my grip. He mumbled and nodded his head, lost in a momentary daze. "I expected cum at the end, but I'm not complaining."

"It makes quite a mess."

I sat up, my hand sweeping a lock from my face. When it fell again, Chelk returned it behind the shell of my ear.

"Next time," I giggled.

"My cocks may be spent but I still have my mouth."

We moved to the bedroom, where he painted me with his tongues. Eventually I had to pull his face away from my cunt. I needed nothing more…couldn't handle anything more. He laughed, pulling me close, both of us feeling warm and sated. Happy. He fell asleep comfortably for the first time without a heavy dose of medication. I memorized the lines and the happy moment. He felt like home.

Chapter Thirty-Two
Painting Anew

Chelk

My favorite goal was preparing Layla's virginal cunt for my cocks. I fought rotha's urges to plow into her and impregnate her without caution. Her body was small and precious, and I refused to hurt her. My incision needed to heal, anyway. Instead, I worked her hot and wet and begging to move to my lap.

In the morning, Layla's curly hair was a frizzy mess atop her beautiful head. Her eyes were sleepy, which made her look adorable. Layla, wrapped in my arms, marked by rotha, gave me contentment I never expected to find again. I suffered major loss…grief, and pain, but I no longer did. I loved Layla, but did she know that? Had I told her that, had I shown her that?

I slipped away and gathered Layla's paintings in the dark. She'd sequestered them in the bedroom, away from areas she deemed communal places. I spent the night redistributing them throughout the house. Rixo helped me in the morning. Now, they reached everywhere, like the love I had for her.

That morning, she wiped her eyes and made her way to kiss Rixo, saying haellea. She noticed one of her paintings hanging behind Rixo, which sent her looking all over the house, just as I'd hoped.

"You got all this done this morning?" she asked.

"No, some last night. Rixo helped." She was already doing the math. For her, any steps were too many. But I was healing, and I wanted to contribute to us now. It had worked. Her eyes cut with concern, but her huge grin overshadowed any scolding.

Rixo grabbed her hand and took her to all the paintings, as he'd curated the collection himself. She tried to stop me as I heated the water for her morning fah, but I encouraged her to finish her tour. She'd enjoyed a hot beverage afterwards. A glance at my unswollen leg convinced her.

She was too sweet for me, like this fah. I added the excessive amount of sweetener she enjoyed. With the mug ready for the hot water, I returned to the "kitchen chair" which had become my active-resting spot. If I took brief breaks, I could get more done. Once my incision healed, I'd be a lot more comfortable. At that point, Arekh would fit me for my prosthesis. My balance, mobility, and stamina would increase from there.

I mourned the end of my military career with anger and sadness, but I'd never aspired to be in the Xavian Guard. My goals were to run and play with Rixo, grow close to my rotha mate, and cook for my community. Hot meals might contribute even more than launching Lian onto the backs of Orkain.

My goals for Rixo were different. I wanted a different world for him—not Earth. Though I'd been a casualty, the Orkain had suffered a tremendous blow.

We'd killed many and scattered them. They'd regroup and plan retribution if possible. Things were coming to a head. We'd see the start and the end of this alien invasion in my lifetime. If we could get rid of them, we could rebuild. How many remained?

I had goals for Layla and me as well: A kumirata and wedding ceremony, and a proposal on bended knee. I wanted to do so, kneeling and rising of my accord. Every day I exercised, practiced, and grew stronger.

Chapter Thirty-Three
One Bed

Layla

I sat on his face, my fingers tracing the curves of his horns. His tongues traveled in many directions, speeding up and slowing down. He listened to my every moan, cued by my breathing and the muscle contractions of my core and even my toes. He learned me. The scruff on his chin and cheeks pricked my thighs as I squeezed. What I thought was one tongue would bloom into two or three, pleasure spread through my core, lighting my body on fire. I came, his tongue thrusting into me, piercing me when I was most tight and sensitive. My body tightened in a second rush of bliss. I whimpered. He lapped tenderly as I relaxed.

He grabbed my cheeks, growling when I attempted to climb off.

"No, not yet. You're not ready," he said.

He licked the wetness from his lips with three swipes of his tongues. Then, pulled me back on top of him.

I groaned in frustration. I've never been patient, and these rotha marks lit a fire under my skin. As his leg healed, he prepared me with his tongues, convinced he'd injure me with his monstrous proportions.

He'd be down there all night if I let him. I wanted him to fill me with cock. I was too horny to wait much longer. He wanted everything to be perfect before we did *it*. He didn't understand that he was perfect, which made this perfect. My mind chased the many possibilities; I rocked on his face and came again, almost to my frustration.

As a compromise, I spun around to face what I wanted. I yanked his underwear down his legs. Long cocks with heads not unlike human penises greeted my hand. Unlike human cocks, they were velvety soft, lubricating, and prehensile. I fought the eager smile on my lips to kiss them.

Into my mouth I drew the smallest of the three, sucking. My hands braced myself on his still solid legs.

"I want," I said.

"One more time," he claimed.

I ground on his face, agitated and anxious until he found the spot. The back of his tongues glided on my clit. All but desire evaporated. My thighs heated his horns and clenched tight. He hummed into and through me, turned on by my satisfaction. My core tightened before releasing tendrils of ecstasy in every direction. I soaked his tongues. He pressed his tongues inside me, licking eagerly at my juices.

I peeled away from him, electricity crawling pleasurably up my spine. I positioned his smallest cock against my swelling slit. We moved smoothly together. He pawed at my body, squeezing my breasts and plying me with his members. Our legs entwined, my feet far from his.

I came back to him and tilted against his cocks. He played with my clit and worked himself gradually inside me. Even his smallest was large, and the sensation was overwhelming. I tightened and tensed.

"Relax, I'm okay," he said when he caught me looking at his stump.

Chelk's hands caressed down my sides, along my hips and thighs, relaxing me. I pulled myself up and got lower with my next stroke. He supported my legs easily with hands, so I could comfortably take my time. He continued to massage my clit, my body melting like butter.

Both full and weightless, he played inside me like an ocean wave. Not even fully seated, he filled me. This was amazing. My pussy pulsed. He rubbed faster as my pussy pulsed in orgasm. I muttered obscenities, coming down from a new peak.

True to his word, he loved hearing me cum. Without changing the pace, he pumped intensely. He gritted his teeth. "Layla," he whispered through them. The cocks smothered between us shuddered. I expected to feel liquid everywhere, but there wasn't any.

"Did you?" I asked.

"I…couldn't help it. You felt spectacular. You're beautiful."

"I thought you'd ejaculate this time."

"This was about you, not me."

I pressed kisses against his skin as I climbed down, nestling beside him. Amazing. I hadn't been able to handle much, but at least tonight it had been enough for Chelk, too.

I looked forward to more.

Chapter Thirty-Four
Divine Dining

Chelk

Everything about Layla subverted my expectations and left me in wonder. Our first sex acts left me shuddering, anxious to impregnate her. This relationship encompassed more than lust and desire. I fought to catch us up.

Under the guise of creating a menu palatable to both Xavian and human, I paraded many tastes in front of Layla for her approval. She shared her preferences and pointed out dishes that might be difficult to scale. She was correct there. I would not stuff pasta shells with my rotha mate's favorite flavors and textures for everyone. Just for her.

I pieced together the perfect meal from everything she enjoyed. Besides the perfect menu, I needed the perfect time. That was difficult when we had Rixo. Layla would suspect something if I arranged childcare. I aspired to be more subtle. So I kept the perfect meal's ingredients stocked and fresh, waiting for the perfect evening. Rixo's inconsistent sleep schedule created many false starts, yet this evening offered hope.

Layla read *The Tiny Saf* to sleepy-eyed Rixo. I wasn't sure who liked the book more: Layla or Rixo. I'd been asking around about future saf litters for her. Layla often spoke about how much she loved animals. Delaying was difficult; I wanted to gift her everything instantly. Instead, I hoped for a lifetime of giving.

I tucked a bottle of fage and Layla's book under my arm and held the empty glass. With one leg, it was easier to pour the drink closer to her. I didn't recognize the book. Neither Kaytor nor I read such silly romances. She must have borrowed it from someone.

"I know," she said with a devious smile.

I blinked. She did?

"We shouldn't let him sleep right now."

Oh, she didn't know. He snoozed, nestled under her arm.

"No, let him sleep."

I handed her the book and poured her a glass.

"Are you learning about Xavian sex?" I joked in a hoarse whisper.

"In my medical books, yes. Human women are simple."

I shrugged. I enjoyed how good we were together.

"What are we having for dinner?" She asked, judging whether she should risk waking Rixo to help me.

"Don't worry. I'll pull something together," I shrugged again, trying to play it off, before disappearing into the kitchen.

The pre-cut dough rose to room temperature while I cut her favorite vegetables into perfect, same-sized cubes before sauteing them.

I sweated, and not from standing over the stove. Layla hadn't grown up the way I did, with knowledge of rotha. She could reject it and leave on the next rocket off this planet. She didn't have many choices, but she had choices. And my rattling bones respected that. I considered making noise and waking Rixo to sabotage my plans.

I adjusted the heat. The pan had gotten too cold. If the dumplings didn't crust, they'd turn to mush in the sauce. I'd hide any burst ones on my plate.

I'd pulled it off—a meal my love would love. Now for the scary part…could Layla get out from underneath Rixo without waking him?

Layla solved that problem.

"Looks like it's only the two of us tonight," she said, coming up behind me.

Chapter Thirty-Five
Cinderella

Layla

I had surprised him. His dinner setting surprised me. I brightened. Chelk had already assumed it would be only the two of us. There was no setting for Rixo. Dangerous, sharp blades and glass mingled with burning candles I didn't know he had. He'd plated a dinner of fish katsu with a creamy sauce and dumplings.

Was this some sort of date?

Chelk pulled out my seat and pushed me in with the leverage of his left leg. He moved around well and was healing. I stopped trying to do everything and even stopped worrying sometimes. We could be partners with regular give and take.

"Wow, this looks wonderful," I said, amazed.

He cooked this while I read on the urish?

"A new dish for you to try. I hope you enjoy them," he said with a lopsided grin.

I cut into one dumpling. It burst with pichini and bright purple root vegetables.

They melted in my mouth. They were fucking delicious. I might have groaned. "Mmm, this is amazing."

I ate slowly, savoring and enjoying it. The dim lights hid Rixo's clutter. He kept pouring the fage. It was all rather romantic.

"What's going on?" I asked.

Was this a special occasion? One of my Xavian birthdays? He was right; they came often. I had given up on them. Still, this dinner had all my favorite things and some things I hadn't yet known were my favorite.

He didn't answer my question. He only smiled.

"This is amazing. Definitely my favorite meal, but there's no way you can serve this en masse," I said.

The dumplings must take forever to stuff.

"You're right, but I can cook it for you. I'd cook it for you happily every day for the rest of our lives," he said.

Chelk got out of his chair and stooped on his busted leg. What was this? We were already rotha mates, weren't we? This was a human tradition, although he didn't have a ring.

"I want to be with you. Not because you are my rotha mate, not because you make my life easier, but because I love you. I choose to love you and be with you. Will you love me and be with me?" he asked.

Sitting, I was closer to being level with him. Between hugs, I stroked his horns and hair. He didn't speak of rotha. He spoke of us—him and me.

"Yes. Of course. I love you." I said into his ear, tracing my fingers over the similar curves of my own. Odd how similar we were. Odd how closely we fit together. Or maybe not odd. We were rotha mates, after all. Chelk said that rotha wasn't everything…that instead, I was everything. "I choose to be with you too. No matter what happens—come spaceship or Orkain. I will always choose to be here with you, over everything else."

He gazed into my eyes. "Well, that's good, because you might kill me over dessert."

"Dessert?" I asked, more eager for sugar than the lifetime of sweetness promised by Chelk.

He laughed. "You light up like Rixo when I mention treats. It must be how you stay so sweet. I do have something else for you."

From underneath my seat, he pulled a pair of fleecy shoes with a padded sole. They were shoes for me!

"Oh, thank you!" I pulled one to my chest and examined it. He put the other one on my foot. A perfect fit! I'd been wearing out my socks on the hard floor. These would be much more comfortable.

"It fits like Cinderella." He remembered that fairy tale I'd told Rixo…and I guessed him. Instead of getting a ring, I got a slipper.

"They fit because you had them made for me."

I loved them even more.

He then reached underneath the seat and pulled out a pair of boots for outdoor wear.

"I had Gulshan make you more socks, too. I want you to be warm since I only have one limb to keep your feet warm at night. And I wanted you to have spares, and I thought this design looked nice."

He pulled out two more pairs of shoes. This was more than I needed. One pair of shoes, or simply reminded me to speak with Gulshan, was all I needed. He took care of me, and I had a pile of custom-made shoes.

"Do you like them?" he asked sincerely.

I loved them. After I marveled at the stitching, he put the slippers on both my feet. I walked and spun in them, happy.

"That's all of them, right?" I laughed, pulling him up from his kneeling position.

The pile of socks and shoes reminded me of Christmas—a small fortune. We settled on the chair. I sat on his lap, leaning on his left leg. My arms wrapped around him.

"Oh, and dessert," he said.

"In a minute."

I kept him off balance and close. I admired my shoes, and I admired my mate. He constantly chose me. We chose to be together.

"Anytime, my sunshine." His hands fell around my waist. "Forever."

Dessert was a fruit sorbet with fresh fage leaves. The flavors danced on my tongue. I could eat gallons of it. However, the bulge in Chelk's pants greatly distracted me. Before he'd finished his serving, my hand traveled the impressive V of muscles to his pants.

Dessert plates never made it to the sink. I did blow out the candles, though. We shuffled to our bedroom, using furniture to support him and our making out. I sat him on the bench at the foot of the bed.

Too impatient, I didn't loosen his pants enough. He helped me fight them over his hips. We cleared his underpants too. His three green cocks wagged…fucking waved at me. How did those ever fit inside me?

I gathered my skirt, hiked it over my hips, and sat on his lap. He assisted me with my damp panties before leaning back onto the foot of the bed. I trailed kisses up his abs, his chest, to his neck.

"Let me taste you," he said greedily as he pulled me up to his face.

I was wet and needy. My toes curled, thighs tightened around his horns. Like a tremble that only escaped at the farthest reaches of my control, I came.

"Is that all I'm allowed?" He asked when I pulled away from him.

Yeah, it was all that he was allowed because I wanted him to fill me with cock. Any cock would do. He seated one of his heads against my opening.

He was large, and the sensation was overwhelming. I tightened and tensed. Chelk remained stationary and reminded me to breathe.

"Do you want this?" His mouth was still close enough to kiss.

I thrust at him. "Yes," I moaned. More than wanting it, I needed it. I didn't know what I'd do without it.

He pressed gently into me, and my world slowly came undone. He pumped in and out of me.

"Oh, look at my good girl taking my cock."

I clenched, my entire body tensing around him. When my spasm relaxed, he was able to pull out of me.

"I think you're ready for the next size."

What? This one was plenty, but Cassie had explained to me that the center cock was the best because it left the shorter, top one to play against the clit. True to their word, Chelk pushed inside and rubbed my stretched front. With only a few thrusts, I orgasmed again. His thick member pulsing as I cried out into his chest.

"I love being inside you. You feel so good," he grunted.

He rested momentarily, but a hungry look remained. He gave me kisses on all the skin he could reach. I felt sensitive all over. It only left me wanting more. Chelk read me, stretching inside me. He found a spot that sent shivers up my spine, teasing it with his thick head.

Fuck. I welcomed the movement, arching my hips toward him as if he needed any help. Meanwhile, he pressed on my clit, rubbing in sync. His eyes spun faster, and his grip tightened. I soaked him in as he shuddered, his glistening muscles, his lips curled in ecstasy. I enjoyed being the source of his satisfaction.

A wave of pleasure crashed into me. My hips locked in place and my body tensed against his as he held me close. He slipped out and perused my clit again. I quivered with aftershocks I'd never experienced. He hugged me and kissed the top of my head.

He slipped back in, steely hard. I shuddered over his massive cock, stuffed. I wasn't sure I could cum again, but he rocked slowly and massaged me. Finding room to move, I dragged my body over his ridges. He grabbed a handful of my hair and breast, playing with my nipple in his fingers. I wrapped my arms around his arm, using it as leverage, riding him. He got harder and larger. His powerful hands pushed my body onto his needy cock. He twisted inside me, searching for that spot. I cried out that I didn't want him to stop. He was close, too.

"Cum inside me," I pleaded, my legs grabbing his muscled sides, fully seated.

"You want me to finish? You want to see how much you've encouraged?" he asked, piercing deep inside me.

He unlocked a new place inside me. I was beyond feeling shy. I was daring and willing. I'd take all three of his cocks if I wasn't already at the edge. I wanted his babies too, because he was everything I wanted. Our love would create a new life and love.

"Yes, cum for me."

He grunted his approval and fucked me with more deep strokes before shooting cum. My core shook and shuddered with fiery pleasure. A tingling sensation spread through my limbs, through my fingers and the knuckles of my toes. I sucked on his fingers to stifle my cry as I came. My entire body pulsed on top of him before I collapsed. My hair covering his face, probably my curls tangling in his horns, but I didn't care—spent and warm. His arms rested heavy on me. We both panted softly.

"I will give you anything I can," he said.

"I thought there'd be more cum," I giggled.

"You want all that? Then you'll have to learn to take more…" he said suggestively.

We had a lifetime to practice. I inhaled our combined scent and fell asleep in his warmth.

Chapter Thirty-Six
Kumirata

Layla

Kumiratas didn't have the tradition of white dresses, nor did Gulshan have a lot of white bright fabric, so I picked out a deep wine color. He spent three weeks working on my dress, which was too much for one occasion, but he wasn't deterred. He hadn't been able to do something so fancy since Sara's dress. Before then? Before the invasion. I'd never been fitted for attire. Now, the drape of my dress and my shoes fit me perfectly.

Chelk worked hard as well. He created a special menu for our kumirata. While we couldn't have a big gathering, he wanted to deliver food and fage to our "guests" in their homes. We could share the same meal and be part of a larger community, even if the Orkain kept us physically apart. Providing everyone in Xavia who desired the packaged meal was an intense ordeal and a multi-day process. Chelk cooked up a storm and loved every minute.

Cassie and Zade arrived to help. Zade voiced the food idea was silly, but he helped Chelk deliver it.

Cassie helped me get dressed and helped wrangle little Rixo, who was constantly underfoot.

"This color is beautiful on you," she said for the third time as she buttoned the long row of wine fabric-covered buttons that added detail to the back and an extra three days of hand-sewing.

"Thank you," I worried my hair might fall from my up-do or if I'd be nervous saying my vows in front of the settit. Many people had joined.

"You're nervous! Stop! It's like an online meeting from back home. Don't even look at them. It's me, Zade, and your future husband," she said.

"Chelk doesn't like the word *husband*. He likes rotha mate more."

"It is a weird word…huzz-band." Cassie agreed, shrugging.

All the buttons were done, and she set me loose. I admired the dress more than I admired myself in the mirror. Gulshan did an amazing job draping the fabric to highlight my favorite curves. I almost missed my curly hair. With straightness, I felt stiff.

"We're back!" announced Chelk.

"Gulshan made this for me. Isn't it pretty?"

"Not nearly as pretty as you," he smirked. Rixo climbed into his arms, and they whooped and hollered.

The two matched. Gulshan made them vests from the same wine-colored fabric as my dress. Chelk wore another, larger, darker vest on top to break up the color, and he looked fabulous, showing off his muscular arms and chest.

"All right, let's get married so we can eat!" I said, eager to squash the butterflies in my stomach.

Drex directed the kumirata, first thanking us for Chelk's sacrifice. Chelk's pant leg covered his prosthetic, but that was old news overshadowed because he was the best cook in Xavia. Drex held up fage delivered by Chelk or Zade and toasted the couple marked to be together forever. Kumiratas were more party than ceremony, but Chelk and I exchanged a few promises.

"My first months here were an enormous change. Moto was kind, and moving away from him was a giant risk. You and little Rixo have changed everything. It's a risk to live on Xavia, but I want to do it with you. Whatever else there is, I'll be there, too. I want to be with you always. And you too, Rixo."

Rixo grinned beside his father in his cute little vest. He ran off and didn't even upend the settit.

I couldn't predict what Chelk would share. He was rather private.

"I will love you forever. I've loved you forever. Everything leading up to here was for this moment and every moment still to come."

Don't cry. He thinks all this heartbreak brought me? I hoped never to let him down. Impossible, but rotha promised a lifetime of opportunity. Kumirata was only a formality. Our time together had already begun. We shared a kiss, and somewhere in the room, Rixo whooped.

Still on the settit, we moved to the table. While Chelk could move deftly, now sitting, his hands shook. He didn't talk in front of many in either of his jobs.

"Tell me about the food," I said, putting my hand on his.

He looked down at my tiny one and covered it with his own. And then he did. He fed me each piece and explained what he wanted them to represent. The first was brack with different toppings, like bruschetta. He included different flavor profiles to represent the many things we would go through together—sweet happiness, sour fear, bitter disgust, salty anger, umami sadness, and the surprise of bubbly fage. Like life, it was a mixture of flavors and sensations. We'd ride the emotions of life together. Rotha marks were icing on the cake. Actually, they were the icing on the cake. He decorated the tiny cakes with our striped marks. Well, tried.

"You can teach me how to paint," he said.

"You can teach me how not to burn the pichini."

"No matter what, you've brought sunshine into my life. You've brought sunshine into the lives of so many on Xavia."

Cassie nodded, glossy-eyed, to confirm. I hadn't seen her cry since she was pregnant with Cash. She and Zade might need to practice with two kids sooner than later.

He continued. "You not only find beauty with your paintings; you find positivity in every single day. Even when I don't think it exists, you bring hope. You bring me hope, Layla. I'm clinging onto that hope."

The sweetness of the cake upended an evening of sweetness. After dessert, another toast with the bubbly fage, and a last kiss, we turned off the broadcast.

Chelk let out an enormous sigh that made everyone laugh. It was weird to make such pomp and circumstance, especially when we couldn't gather, but someday it would be different. We'd return to the sun. Chelk surprised me by speaking to everyone about our love. He joked that he'd become more mindful now that he'd lost his limb. I'd encouraged him to stop hiding behind his big soldier body and express more.

I reached out to give Chelk a peck on the cheek. He lowered himself , allowing for the kiss. He came back up, rosy in the cheeks.

"What was that for?" he asked.

I hoped my eyes conveyed what I wished. *Him.* Later.

It took him a moment before he caught on, but the way his hand trailed on my hip as he walked back into the kitchen to make-nice with Zade was telling. Rotha love was forever-love and baby-love all tied into one. Cassie and Zade took Rixo for a few nights. We felt a little guilty, but Zade and Cassie lived in one of the safest homes. Once shooed from our home and safe inside theirs, we cuddled and fell asleep on the urish for an hour.

Well, I slept for an hour. Chelk somehow escaped from underneath me. When I awoke, he'd transformed the place with red-tinted lights and flickering candles. Nothing we'd be able to have with Rixo running around.

"Ah, I set up a bath for you."

There wasn't a toy in sight. I didn't ruin the illusion by opening the closet. Instead, I counted the flower petals as they floated past me and sipped on the glass of fage until the steam and drink had me feeling loopy.

"I love the dryer," I said, coming out fresh, wearing only the long, loose nightshirt he'd left for me.

"You love everything," he said.

Maybe he was right. We didn't have them on Earth, so I appreciated them. I appreciated him, too. There was no one like Chelk on Earth.

I expected a veritable feast on the table, like what happened every time I left Chelk unattended in the kitchen. He'd think he was feeding the Xavian Guard and pile food on plates. The table was clean without a single setting.

"We will dine in the bedroom tonight," he said mischievously.

What was this man up to? I hadn't felt comfortable asking Katy or Sara about their kumirata nights. They'd only told me that things were pleasantly reversed in their culture. In Xavian tradition, Kumirata night was the man's responsibility. What did that mean? I didn't know, but I was about to find out.

I let Chelk lead me down the hall. The bedroom was full of mood lighting, too dark to see.

"How are we going to eat like this?" I asked, giggling.

He shushed me and motioned for me to lie on the bed. Above me, a facsimile of a starry sky was there to occupy my eyes.

"Tonight I eat you and what you feed me. You are my dinner."

"They're ticklish," I warned as he started at my feet, but he held them firmly, grazing kisses on my toes, ankles, and calves.

He separated my legs, making room for himself, pushing my nightshirt up to my waist. I relished his rough lips on my rotha marks, which tingled pleasurably. He nibbled my inner thighs, teasing me with his tongues. Heat radiated from him. His full attention was enthralling. I buzzed with energy. I feared I'd explode at the first touch of my clit, but worse, he stopped. "Oh yes, I forgot *your* dinner."

"Sorry, what?" I said, floating in a bit of a daze, only aware he was no longer edging me along.

Instead, he came north. Pinched between his fingers was a sliver of *something* for me to eat. I cut my eyes at him. "What is this?"

"It's the flavor I want in your mouth when you cum for the first time tonight. It's the appetizer."

My eyes widened, and I stuck out my tongue obediently. Hard like candy, but not sweet. It was zesty with a cooling menthol effect. Damn, I tingled with each graze of his lips as he traveled down my body to make me cum before the taste faded from my mouth. Finally, his mouth was on my pussy, feasting with all three tongues.

Chapter Thirty-Seven
Senses

Chelk

Controlling and caring for all of Layla's senses as I feasted on her hardened my dicks. I could eat like this for the rest of my life. And I could make sure Layla ate well, too. When she came from her daze, she reached for vyg, a juicy, messy fruit, not unlike her. She fed it to me as I lay between her legs, if only to distract my mouth and give herself a break. Her break didn't last long as I licked the vyg juices off her heat. My thoroughness gave way to hand squeezing my horn, thighs clenching my head, and her sweet mouth squealing my name. Her taste was unmatched. I brought the nectar to her mouth.

"I'm glad you chose the vyg," I said, replacing myself with the fruit. Her lips wrapped around its delicate skin excited me. I kissed the juice from her chin before attending to my prosthetic. I didn't need the leverage, and it would only rub and make me sore.

"Why? What's the vyg stand for?" she asked.

Layla had caught on that all my food preparations, in ceremony or in sex, had reasons.

"It's what I want in your mouth when I enter that perfect ass of yours."

Layla's eyes got as big as the vyg which dropped from her mouth. Turns out I still had some surprises for her. We'd talked about it, and I'd been playing and prepping my virgin's ass.

"We can work our way up to the vyg." I laughed and caught the tumbling fruit.

I dribbled syrup onto her chest to lick up. She giggled, her hands in my hair, keeping it safe from the stickiness. Once I'd cleaned her up and sucked her nipples into taut peaks, I pulled close against her entrance. Entwining my tongues with hers, I hoped she caught notes of the sweet syrup as I pushed into her sweet pussy.

I focused on the twists of her small, soft body, determined not to cum instantly inside her throbbing tightness. Fuck, she was tight. I found the spot that made her squirm, rubbed her clit with a free cock, and rimmed her with the third. I loved making her cum. She grabbed at the sheets, and then, her arm reached out and grabbed for the vyg.

So much for taking our time. As her body relaxed, I pulled my thick, slick cock from her and readied my smaller one at her puckered hole. Guided by her breaths and encouraging her with another orgasm, I let her tightness draw me in. The ring of pressure was hot, and by the grace of the stars, I didn't cum. I focused on her, petting her, and pulling the vyg from her mouth. She kept a bite and chewed, taking two cocks at once. I praised her.

While not part of the menu, I dunked two fingers into the syrup and shoved them in her mouth. Her lips and jaws contorted to accommodate. My girl looked so pretty with all of her holes filled. Fryyre. That did it. I released from my free cock, squirting ropes of hot cum on her clit, up her stomach, breasts, face, curls, the bed, headboard, and wall. She clenched around me.

"Fuck," she cried as I rubbed. Her body arched into mine, my seed between us. "I want you to cum inside me."

Part of it was rotha—it made you want to fucking breed. It upped everything, rotha marks like go-lights on your love. But I wasn't on its or any rushed timeline. This was her kumirata night.

"Oh, I will, but not yet," I hummed in her ear, glad I had the choice.

If she could form full sentences, I wasn't finished. I would take her to the brink over and over and then fill her with my seed. Every sense of hers would buzz and beg for mercy before I pumped my seed into her womb.

True to my word, I fucked my sweet sunshine into oblivion. She begged again, squatting obscenely on my cocks. I stroked deep and slow, thinking about her swell with my offspring. Agreeably, I slipped the final food into her mouth. Her eyes widened and lips puckered as she sucked on the still sour Helena berries. The first of the season.

"For when I put this baby inside you."

"Jesus!" she exclaimed. Her face lit up.

"We can talk about names later," I grunted, so close.

She gave a laugh before falling back into rhythm. I pressed her down when she threatened to slip off, her pussy tight. All the edging had me nearly bursting.

Fryyre. Her channels milked my shaking cock, rocking me between enjoyment and too much. My cum overfilled her and soaked us both. This woman was mine. From her marks on the outside to the baby that would grow inside her…all of her, her transformations from this lifetime to the next would forever be mine. I rubbed her clit and made her pussy tremble still inside her.

Epilogues

Layla

The barley and butter beans steamed in a huge vat set upon a stove barely large enough for it. Chelk's delivery meals had been such a tremendous success. I'd never seen him happier, even as he chased Rixo out of the kitchen for the thirteenth time, fake-swatting his booty with his prosthetic.

A faint cry emerged from the other room.

"Don't mess with Kayla," Chelk warned, realizing both our children were unsupervised.

"I'm not; she's hungry," called Rixo.

I didn't need to retrieve our baby. Rixo brought her to me. Rixo held her with the confidence of an older brother. He'd tripled in height. He still called me Lala. Her chubby yellow-green cheeks and pink lips scrunched up in a super-serious baby face. Rixo handed her over to me. I smoothed her wispy hair on her head and set her up to nurse. Whether she'd call me Lala or Mommy was still uncertain. She heard Lala more often than not.

"Thank you, Rixo," I said.

He bothered his father again and Chelk required we leave the kitchen before he dished the food.

"I'm bored," complained Rixo, staring up at me and his little sister to be entertained.

"I'm sorry. Why don't you read your sister a story while she eats?" I fell onto an empty spot on the couch. I hoped to entertain both children from there.

Surprisingly, Rixo pulled out *The Tiny Saf* and climbed onto the couch next to us. He petted his sister's head. "I'm going to read to you."

Reading was generous. Rixo had the story memorized. At least, he turned the pages at the right time. He only unintentionally smacked his sister twice with the book. I might have fallen asleep. The children had been on different nap schedules. Caring for them and helping to cook for ten to fifteen people exhausted me. It would only get more chaotic when Kayla started walking. Rixo was a toddler when I met him. Motherhood for someone as tiny as Kayla was new, but Rixo and Chelk had been a great help.

Chelk loaded the food containers into his satchel. He planted a kiss on my lips, nuzzled the top of Kayla's head, and then balanced expertly as he pried Rixo off his side.

"Can I go with you?" he pleaded, like he always did.

"Not yet. When you get older."

"I'm older now."

We both laughed. "That's true."

When Rixo got older, he could go with Chelk, but for now the route was too long and he was too young. They'd get quality time together and Rixo would be of wonderful help.

I returned to the kitchen, which never seemed to empty. From fah in the morning, lunch, meal preparation for deliveries, to late dinner—the kitchen remained busy. Even late at night Chelk would make me fah as I nursed Kayla. I dished out barley and butter beans for Rixo and me. Kayla ate a few mouthfuls too. After Rixo's bath, we argued about bedtime.

"But hah-zah's not home yet!"

"That doesn't mean it's not bedtime. I'll make sure he says goodnight to you when he comes home." I checked the time again. Chelk was late, but not worryingly late. He'd probably got stuck chatting with Davian or helping someone.

Rixo and Kayla fell asleep in the nursery in their own beds for once. Chelk wasn't even there to celebrate with me. He really was late. After cleaning the kitchen, I pulled out my paint supplies out of habit. I was finishing a baby gift for Dani and Moto, their child's name Ella in large cursive print and flowers that bloomed when she was born. Thankfully, I never had to return to Moto and our crazy pact. Moto and Dani bonded as rotha mates, too. Sara wasn't a bad matchmaker at all.

After putting Rixo to bed, I called Cassie. I told her about Chelk being late.

"I can't say why, but I think he's okay."

Oh my gosh. How Cassie kept her pregnancy secret for so long was mind-boggling. I could see right through her.

"What do you know?!" I asked.

"Oh, nothing," she said in a faux-innocent way. I could tell it was nothing bad. She didn't want me to worry.

"What's going to happen?" I asked.

I liked surprises, but I liked spoiled surprises even more. She knew something good was happening.

"I won't ruin it," she said, her eyes glistening.

"Okay, fine. Keep your secrets."

I sorted the information she might know. How were they keeping this secret from me?

"Settit me later!" she said chirped.

I laughed and said haellea. I should ask Chelk if it's 'calling' or 'settiting.' *Where was he?* I poured myself a glass of fage and sat on the urish, paintings abandoned. I was determined to relax.

There was nothing to worry about…

Chelk

The rain fell in chilly lines between myself and my backpack filled with roasted vegetables and steamed nuts. My prosthetic slid on the damp leaves and got stuck in the mud. Something with a larger surface area closer to my natural foot-size would be better for this terrain and weather. If I remembered, I'd tell Tess, Arekh's assistant, later today. I'd meet her, but not for a prosthetic modification. Those meetings had become less frequent after they'd designed the prosthetic I wore. Losing my leg had been difficult, but it had also been an opportunity. I quit fighting. I cooked with a purpose. And I didn't merely cook. I delivered hearty meals to those in need.

My first stop was for Davian, the busy communications officer. If I left the food on his doorstep, he'd sometimes forget. I no longer accepted an unanswered knock, either. I had gotten a spare key from him and delivered the food onto his kitchen counter. Today, the rain kept him inside. His place was like my own, but I forgot how bare walls looked. Two resident artists had covered my house in colorful paintings and drawings. Any papers he had were on horizontal surfaces, full of schematics and maps of the villages and tunnels. It was a dizzying amount of information. I'm glad I wasn't one to keep up with all of that.

We exchanged haellea, and I turned and stooped so he could reach the top of my pack. Davian was shrinking and his hair grew silver. It was a rare sight on Xavia, still the era in which he worked probably took its toll.

"How is the baby?" he asked.

"Tiny and strong. Louder than Rixo," I laughed. Despite her delicate frame, she was terribly loud. She soon won over my heart and entire being.

"Sounds like a healthy human all right. When will you have another?"

Davian needed to mind his own business. Layla was still breastfeeding and caring for Kayla. I wouldn't let him rush our family so he could see population numbers blossom under his care.

"Do not push. She is human, not Xavia's Jesus."

Sure, she'd saved my child and changed my life. She created life, hope, and love in places I thought had grown dark long ago. She was my savior, and I'd protect her from any more harm. There were other, less productive families he could bother.

"Who is Jesus?" he asked.

"A superhero on Earth," I explained.

Davian let the subject go as he opened the lid of his food and examined the steamy contents.

"Butter beans…but when will we get more radish?" he asked.

"Moto says we need more sandy soil for radishes. Perhaps next season we'll try to regain the land eastward," I suggested.

Davian picked at his beans, considering the soil quality of territories to be taken from the Orkain. His affinity for radishes might influence tactical decisions. Now out of the military, I knew more than ever before. Gossip could be quite efficient, especially when accompanied by a hot dinner.

"Perhaps. I worry Bonnie lives in that direction."

Like Davian, I had conflicting feelings about Bonnie. I credited her return to the Orkain for my family's safe passage from Heljin's that day. She hadn't taken my leg, but she was a catalyst for the rushed attack. We didn't want to hurt her, but she lived with the enemy.

I rushed through the rest of my deliveries with a special task to complete afterward. I wasn't talented at lying. When I told Layla I was packing extra for Moto and Dani, she put in double. The couple was busy with their newborn and a harvest. Layla had told me about her and Moto's pact. How if they hadn't found happiness elsewhere, they'd return to their living arrangement. Thankfully Moto and Dani were rotha mates, too. Everyone had found their rotha mate. I was glad to be a part of Layla's life. Layla and our family blessed me deeply.

Layla often asked why I didn't trust rotha in the beginning. I wanted her to have her own choice, the best of everything, and didn't think that was me, especially after my injury. I didn't want my disastrous fate to be hers. In ways I don't completely understand, she loves me every day, and I've learned to trust that.

The meals were a gift for Tess, who had a friendly breeding saf pair. Many safs went feral after Xavians released them. They lived on the outskirts, close to safety but no longer good for petting. Layla had been so enamored with the books and the idea of pet ownership. I'd spent well over a year finding her a small saf to call her own.

Tess answered the door with saf hair flying and squeals of terror behind her.

"Come on in," she said, delicately stepping around the chasing beasts. "How is the prosthetic?"

"Slippery on the leaves," I was honest with her. She'd helped design it. "It was great in the dry season, but—"

"Is it getting stuck in the mud all the way here?" She pointed to the mud.

"Uh, yeah," I said as she walked away.

She grabbed a sheet of paper and began sketching.

"I'll make it work for now. I only came for the saf," I said.

"Oh yes, grab any old one." She laughed at her own joke.

I'd paid double for the only orange saf in the litter. He was easy to spot in the streaks of purple. Black fringe had grown on the tips of his ears to match his spots since I'd last seen him. He toppled twice over himself, but overall, he was much more agile. I related.

I swapped out the food dish for the saf, pinching the fur behind its shoulders to lift him. His triangular ears tucked back, and he squeaked his protest. Tess might not have even noticed me leaving. She'd have a prototype for me in a few days, I expected.

In better weather I may have had trouble keeping the saf in the pack but the rain and cold and scariness of the wild outside seemed to keep it tucked safe. Occasionally it mewed.

"You'll be home soon," I cooed over my shoulder.

I hoped it wouldn't hold a grudge. Twice more I sank into the mud.

At home, Layla sat amid painting supplies interspersed with the residual mess that was Rixo and his toys. She jumped to hug me and eyed my muddy prosthetic.

"You're late. Did you fall?" She asked.

"No, dear, I didn't."

I hung my pack and sat down to remove my boot and clean my prosthetic. I'd tell her about the modifications needed later.

"Good," she said, as if her worrying had worked.

I hadn't meant to make her worry. I'd been gone a while if she'd already gotten both children to bed and pulled out her paints.

She stooped to help me with my prosthesis. She didn't need to do so, and she gazed playfully between my legs. It wasn't caretaking; it was intimacy. While difficult at first, my injury ultimately brought us closer. I pulled her into my arms. Her soft curls caught in the crooks of my arms. She nestled her face into my chest, and her body deflated as worry left it. I was home with her.

Then, the saf meowed.

"What was that?" she jumped up. "Did you hear that?"

"Oh," I motioned to the bag beside me, which was rocking ever so gently as the creature pawed. "That's for you." Layla gave me a sharp look, trying to figure out what was going on. "That's why I was late."

She cautiously approached the bag and flipped the top without pulling the bag from the hook. Its little orange face poked out and cried.

Layla shoved her hand into her mouth to deaden her squeal.

"Is that a saf?" she asked.

"A baby one."

"Oh my gosh. This is a baby? He's as big as an adult cat. He's going to get bigger?"

"Yes, much bigger."

She held it like she held Kayla and nuzzled his soft fur. "I thought they were smaller, like in the book."

"Like in the book called *The Tiny Saf?*"

"Oh, right…" she beamed all the same. "Is it really mine?"

"Yes, for you, my love. I doubt the kids would do a good job caring for it. What are you going to name it?"

"Anything but Lala," she groaned, laughing. The simultaneous presence of both always amused me.

Despite Kayla's birth, Rixo remained obsessed with Layla. He continued to call her Lala and also virtually anything he liked. He wanted Kayla to be named Lala, and he'd try to name this saf Lala too.

"What do you say? *In his defense?*" I recalled Layla's phrase. She nodded to confirm. "In his defense, he doesn't know many names."

"I don't know many Xavian names either…" Layla worried.

"I'm sure you'll come up with a fine name." She'd come up with Kayla's name. It was English, but also combined Layla and Kaytor. Layla wanted to honor Rixo's mother.

"Tiny," she whispered to it.

"He will not be…"

"Tiny."

Tiny would be more trouble than his name suggested. Layla's glowing smile made the pain worth it, though. She's not my rotha, but she's mine anyway—and that makes it even sweeter. It makes *this* even sweeter.

While the saf distracted Layla, I glanced at Layla's current canvas. She didn't always let me see what she's working on. She said I'm not gentle enough on her works in progress. Layla had successfully painted Rixo. He held a lumpy potato of a sister. Okay, she was right—I wasn't always encouraging. Her paintings weren't always great, though.

"I'll add Tiny next to them!" she beamed. "Our little family."

I hugged her close. Like Davian, I had thoughts of a large family. But I learned to expect nothing and appreciate everything. Life had unfolded better than I could ever imagine—and much better than Layla could depict in grainy berry paintings.

This was rotha.

* * * * *

Deleted Steamy Scenes

Join Reverie's Revelries and enjoy two deleted steamy
scenes as a special gift

Reverieharwood.com/newsletter-warrior

A Note for You, the Reader

Dearest Reader,

If it wasn't for you, I'd have given up on the Rotha Mates of Xavia. Thank you for welcoming me into your kind and fanatical community. I didn't know you existed, and now I'm home.

I hope *My Alien Warrior* has added romance, steaminess…and, a little escape…to your day. If you liked it, please review it where you like to buy books. Thank you for your support.

To read the next Rotha Mates of Xavia draft before it's published, check out my Ream or Patreon. For announcements, my newsletter is good to join. And if you just want to say hi? Write to me at reverie@reverieharwood.com. Talk to you soon.

Here's to more romance in the universe,
Reverie Harwood
March 17, 2026

Acknowledgments

I would like to especially thank Matt, Manisha, Robert, Zack, Helen, and Shelby. Your encouragement pushed this book to the finish line when I struggled. I hope to do y'all proud.

www.ingramcontent.com/pod-product-compliance
Lightning Source LLC
Chambersburg PA
CBHW032233050726
47591CB00001B/372